Flip Turn

Monique Polak

James Lorimer & Company Ltd., Publishers
Toronto

James Lorimer & Company Ltd. acknowledges the support of the Ontario Arts Council. We acknowledge the support of the Government of Canada through the Book Publishing Industry Development Program (BPIDP) for our publishing activities. We acknowledge the support of the Canada Council for the Arts for our publishing program. We acknowledge the support of the Government of Ontario through the Ontario Media Development Corporation's Ontario Book Initiative.

Cover illustration: Greg Ruhl

The Canada Council | Le Conseil des Arts
for the Arts | du Canada

ONTARIO ARTS COUNCIL
CONSEIL DES ARTS DE L'ONTARIO

National Library of Canada Cataloguing in Publication

Polak, Monique
    Flip turn / written by Monique Polak.

(Sports stories ; 67)
ISBN 1-55028-819-9 (bound) ISBN 1-55028-818-0 (pbk.)

    I. Title. II. Series: Sports stories (Toronto, Ont.) ; 67.

PS8631.O43F53 2004   jC813'.6   C2004-900484-0

James Lorimer & Company Ltd.,
Publishers
35 Britain Street
Toronto, Ontario
M5A 1R7
www.lorimer.ca

Distributed in the United States by:
Orca Book Publishers
P.O. Box 468
Custer, WA USA
98240-0468

Printed and bound in Canada.

Contents

Acknowledgements

Thanks to the swimmers on the Côte des Neiges team who let me watch them train and put up with my questions, and to their coach Tatiana Yelizarova. Thanks also to Christine Archambault of the N.D.G. Y.M.C.A. for the swimming lesson; swimmer Dafna Wisbaum for helping to get me started; swimmers Caitlin Chapman and Anna Roth Trowbridge for reading early drafts of the manuscript; Rina Singh and Claire Rothman for many years of writerly encouragement; Deena Sacks for reading the manuscript and Viva Singer for reading several versions and for never getting tired of listening to me talk about the story. A special thanks to Hadley Dyer, the children's book editor at James Lorimer and Company; to my daughter Alicia for not minding that her mom lives at the computer; and to my husband, Michael Shenker, for his love and wisdom.

For Ma, with love

1

My Mind's Racing

Icurl my toes underneath the starting block. As I bend my knees and lean forward, I take a deep whiff of chlorine. Electric sparks shoot through my legs.

Racing does that to me.

"On your mark, get set …"

The whistle blows and I'm up on my toes, diving into the pool. My arms and legs are stretched out, muscles tight.

I love what comes next: cool water rushing against my hands, and a huge *splash* as the rest of my body makes contact. I glide underneath the water. Everything looks bright and blue; speckles of light shimmer like silvery fish.

But there isn't time to admire speckles or imagine fish. I kick hard to rise up to the surface and move into the front crawl.

My left arm reaches forward, then my fingers pull down to my knees. Right, left … Now I lift my head and breathe. My legs never stop kicking.

Red and blue flags flap overhead. Even they appear to be urging me to push forward, move faster — win.

I resist the urge to check my time. Three chronometers hang near the pool and I must be passing one now. I don't want to lose even a fraction of a second.

Am I in the lead? Up ahead, the water's calm, not rippling

the way it will if someone gets ahead of me.

Right, left, right, then breathe again. I feel someone splashing nearby and kick even harder.

Someone's catching up. I don't have to turn around to know who it is.

Svetlana snorts as she comes up for air. From the corner of my eye, I see her hands slicing through the water.

I try to focus on my stroke. But I can feel Svetlana coming closer. When I take my next breath, I see her face. Her skin looks so pale it's almost transparent; her nose turns up at the end like a ski jump. Her gaze is focused on the other end of the pool.

I push forward. Near the wall, I tuck in my chin and pull my knees to my chest for a flip turn. Svetlana does the same in the next lane.

With my arms stationary, I spin underwater. Then, a second later, I'm right side up again. I push off the wall with my toes and keep kicking.

Svetlana's right next to me now. I push so hard, I feel my lungs burning. When I move faster, she does too.

Left, right, left, breathe. Svetlana keeps her face out of the water just long enough to catch my eye and grin.

With less than a lap left, I have the feeling Svetlana's purposely keeping pace with me — taunting me. I try to push ahead, but can't, and Svetlana knows it. It takes everything I have to maintain my pace.

I focus on the other end of the pool. Six more strokes and I'll be there. Go! I tell myself.

Svetlana snorts again. A mist of water sprays my shoulders and suddenly, she passes me.

When I reach the wall, I tear off my goggles and hurl them into the water. I hate Svetlana! Even more than that, I hate losing!

"Will you relax? Today was only practice," a voice whispers.

Ashley hands me my goggles. She's puffing slightly. She's come in fourth — not that it would bother her.

Ashley's my best friend, but there are times — like now — when her habit of looking on the bright side gets kind of annoying. It doesn't matter to me that this was practice and not a real competition. The thing is: I just wanna win.

2

Picture Perfect

"Victoria, sweetheart, can you get home from the pool on your own today?"

Wow! That's a lot of talking, I thought. Let me count: *Victoria*, that's one, *sweetheart* is two ... she used 13 words in that sentence — definitely the longest sentence she's come up with in weeks.

Lately, my mom has been talking in monosyllables — which is a fancy way of saying she uses mostly short words, and in her case, not many of them.

"Guess what, Mom? I trimmed a third of a second off my time today."

"Good work, dear."

"You know, Mom, I really liked that veggie-tofu loaf Abigail made."

"Uh-huh."

"Can I take money for my bus pass?"

"Sure, honey."

"Mom, I don't know why I keep swimming. Why do I show up for practice six afternoons a week, not to mention the two mornings I wake up at 5:30 for morning practice? Mom, there's this super annoying Ukrainian girl on the team who's faster than me, and I think I have a crush on a guy named Matt..."

Not that I'd tell her any of that.

Not that she'd say anything else besides "Uh-huh" or "Sure, dear."

I've been using that bus pass a lot lately. Before, Mom dropped me off and picked me up from practice, except when she and Dad had to be at some dinner party or something. Plus, she used to come in at least twice a week to catch the end of practice and hang out with the other parents.

I guess there's no point in asking if she's going to officiate at our next meet. That would involve standing up and using a stopwatch — and I don't think she could handle either of those things right now.

These days, Mom mostly lies in bed with her eyes closed and a damp washcloth on her forehead.

"Can I get you anything, Mom?"

"No, thanks."

"How about an aspirin?"

"Not now."

My dad says not to worry. "She'll get over it, Vic. You know how she gets." Then his pager beeps or his cell phone rings, and he's doing another deal. My dad works in commercial real estate, which means he buys and sells office buildings. He has an office of his own downtown, but he doesn't only work from there. Dad works all the time — even when he's home with us.

The thing is, I *don't* know how my mom gets. Sure, she's had the "blues," when she mopes around the house for a few days and refuses to get out of her bathrobe. But she's been like this for over two months now. If you ask me, she's got the *navy blues*.

Once, Mom told me that spring is the hardest time of year for her. When I asked why, she just shrugged. "I suppose I have trouble with things ending," was all she'd say.

Sure, things end in spring — no more slush, no more winter boots … But other things begin — like crocuses and longer afternoons. But things like that don't cheer Mom up. Like yesterday, I picked some purple crocuses from the front garden and put them in a vase on her nightstand.

"You used to pick flowers for me when you were little," Mom said when she saw them. Her eyes got misty and I was afraid she was going to cry. "Before swimming was all that mattered."

Ouch! I hate when she says stuff like that. Shouldn't she be happy I'm into swimming? I mean, I could be doing something worse — like alcohol or drugs — or even shopping. Would she rather I was one of those kids who hung out at the mall? "Swimming isn't all I care about," I told her.

Mom readjusted the washcloth on her head and sighed. "The crocuses are lovely," she said softly.

I know it sounds selfish, but I need my mom to be the way she used to be. The problem is my mom's been acting this way for so long now, I'm beginning to forget how things were.

Everyone thinks my family's got it all. In a way, we do. We have a lot of stuff compared to most people who live in Côte-des-Neiges. Have I mentioned how that's French for "Side-of-Snow"? Some winter mornings, we have so much snow that when you open the front door, a huge pile lands on your toes. Which is why it's wise to wear slippers that time of year.

Almost all the people who live in Côte-des-Neiges are new immigrants, who spent most of their savings getting to Montreal in the first place. Most of them live in the red brick, low-rise apartments that line our neighbourhood streets.

Mom, Dad and I live on Van Horne Avenue, on this one fancy block that doesn't match the rest of the neighbourhood. To be honest, it's kind of embarrassing to live like us. We've got this big, old, grey stone house with more bathrooms than we can use. Some designer helped mom pick the furniture. And Abigail, our housekeeper, cooks and tidies up after us.

Picture perfect. That's what we are. Or used to be...

When I was growing up, there was this photo shop on Victoria Avenue — which is like our Main Street. (My dad used to tell me Victoria Avenue was named after me. I was disappointed when I learned the street had been around a lot longer than I had.) Anyway, the photo shop had a picture of us in their window.

I guess the shop owner figured that if other families saw *us* looking so happy, they'd want to come in and get their pictures taken too.

The photo shows me in front, with my parents behind. Mom had one hand on my shoulder, and Dad's hand was on Mom's shoulder. When the photographer made us pose that way, I remember thinking we must've looked like something from A Barrel of Monkeys. You know the game where the monkeys come in a plastic barrel and the trick is to loop them together so they don't come apart.

Lots of people — even Ashley when I met her in grade four — used to recognize me from that picture.

I laugh when I think about what kind of family shot the photographer could take of us now. I'd be in my bathing cap and goggles, looking totally confused; Mom would have that washcloth on her forehead, and Dad, well that's easy — he'd be on his cell phone.

3

Warm Up

N'entrez pas — don't go in there!" Madame Lalonde called out.

Madame Lalonde's our coach. You can't blame her for mixing up languages. The kids on our team speak a total of seven: French, English, Arabic, Chinese, Spanish, Russian and Tagalog, which is what they speak in the Philippines.

Madame Lalonde was standing in the lobby of the sports complex. At first, I didn't recognize her. I'm used to seeing her in her blue swimsuit — the one we all wear, with CDN in big yellow letters on the right hip. Today, she was wearing a red track suit and sunglasses.

Ashley and I were about to go through the turnstile into the sports complex, a tricky maneuver when you're carting around a backpack full of school books. What is it about teachers that they always give us so much homework on Mondays?

"We're doing warm-ups outside," Madame Lalonde said, lifting her chin in the direction of Van Horne Park, just outside the complex. "It's too nice to stay indoors."

She was right. It was a perfect spring day in Montreal — warm, not hot like it gets in summer — with a light breeze that tickles you. The crab apple trees were in full bloom, their silvery-pink flowers shimmering against the sky.

That didn't stop us from complaining about having to go outside. I guess people get used to their routines. For us, that means going through the turnstile, showing the receptionist our pool cards, rushing to the locker room, slipping on our swimsuits, pulling on our caps, doing our stretches on the deck, and then — usually with some prodding from Madame Lalonde — diving in.

I could do it in my sleep. In fact, I do, since so many of my dreams are about swimming.

"Do we have to?" Ashley asked, rolling her eyes.

"Do we?" I added.

"Just go," Madame Lalonde said, ignoring us.

Except for Matt, the other kids were already outside gathered around Clara, our new assistant coach. Clara's a phys. ed. student at McGill University, who's writing her thesis — that's like a hundred page term paper — about swim team dynamics.

Ashley and I tossed our backpacks into the pile already on the ground.

"You've been doing great," I heard Clara tell Yvonne, this new girl on our team. I don't know why Clara fusses so much over the weakest swimmers. Yvonne's nice, but let's just say she swims more like a turtle than a fish.

Speaking of fish, after practice last week, a few of us were discussing what we think about during laps. I was surprised by how many kids said they sing to themselves. Had I joined an underwater choir or a swim team? I liked Matt's answer. "I think about being a barracuda," he'd said.

I think about that too. Not being a barracuda, but being a fish — one with shiny stripes to suit my hair, which is blonde and curly — except when it's wet.

When it's wet, my hair is as straight as Matt's, only not as dark. We joined swim team at the same time — four years ago, when we were both nine — but it wasn't until recently that I started noticing Matt's hair — and how cute he is altogether.

"One of the things that makes a swim team special," Clara was saying, looking at each of us as she spoke, "is how you all compete, and cooperate. Each of you wants to be the fastest, but you also want your teammates to succeed."

That wasn't necessarily true, I thought, glancing over at Svetlana.

"I don't really care about being the fastest," Ashley said softly, as if she were thinking out loud. "I just want to do my best. Besides, swimming's good for us."

Ashley's mom made her join the team after she learned Ashley had asthma. Ashley used to have awful asthma attacks, but the steady breathing during swimming helps. She still uses an inhaler during allergy season, but at least now her asthma is under control.

"I vant to be zee fastest," Svetlana announced, straightening her spine as she spoke.

She took the words out of my mouth — minus the accent.

Two little kids stopped climbing the jungle gym to watch us. You could tell they were wondering what a bunch of big kids were doing there. "Don't worry," I called out to them, "the equipment's all yours."

They didn't answer, but they must've heard me, because they went back to playing.

Wouldn't it be fun to climb the jungle gym, play on the swings and try the teeter-totters? Just to be a kid again, and not have to worry about winning or even doing our best. But that wasn't the sort of warm-up Madame Lalonde had in mind.

"Three hundred jumping jacks! Let's go! We have no time for fooling around!" Madame Lalonde called out, clapping her hands as she jogged over in our direction.

We formed a circle around her. In the distance, I could see Matt approaching.

"Over here, baalshahyah reeba!" Svetlana beckoned as her arms spread open and she jumped into the air.

"What did you just call me?" Matt asked Svetlana, punching her arm lightly, as he found a spot between us.

"Baalshahyah reeba," Svetlana repeated. "Zat means *big fish* in Russian. Like Barracuda. Barracuda, ees Russian, too, you know," she said.

"*Baal-shah-yah reeba*." Matt said. "I like that."

But I didn't. Not one bit.

4

Going the Distance

Forty laps!" Madame Lalonde shouted, before we'd even had a chance to catch our breath.

Except for Juan. He hadn't even broken a sweat. Juan worked hard at competitions, but goofed off during warm-ups and practices. When Madame Lalonde's back was turned, he collapsed on the ground, instead of doing proper push-ups.

Oh well, I thought, that's just Juan.

My arms burned. I'd given those push-ups everything I had. That was just me.

The 40 laps Madame Lalonde was talking about weren't in the pool; they were round the park. That's pretty tough if you weren't used to running — and we weren't.

"You seem grumpy," Ashley said as we jogged past the baseball diamond.

"Yeah — thanks to Svetlana," I whispered, turning my head to make sure Svettie wasn't nearby. "Matt likes her."

"Of course Matt likes her," Ashley said, which didn't exactly cheer me up. "Just not the way he likes you," she added, puffing as she spoke. "Tell me. Have you ever seen Matt grab Svettie's foot in the pool?"

"I don't think so," I answered, trying to remember the times I'd seen them together in the water. "But he grabbed *my* foot again Saturday morning."

"You'd better watch out, Vic. Foot-grabbing in the pool is one thing. Next, he'll be grabbing both feet at that bowling party on Friday night."

"Do you really think so?" I asked.

Ashley laughed — at me, I think, for taking her seriously — but then her laugh turned into a raspy cough.

"You okay?" I asked, slowing down and reaching out to pat her back.

"I'm fine. Jogging's hard on my lungs," she said, clearing her throat. "I need to walk a bit. You keep going or Madame Lalonde will have a fit."

Sure enough, when I looked out across the baseball field, Madame Lalonde was glaring in our direction. You'd think we were about to rob a bank. How come she never seemed to notice when Juan was goofing off?

Of course, you couldn't blame Madame Lalonde for being tough. That's what coaches get paid for — helping us improve our technique — and our times.

My times had slowed down since I got my period last year. Madame Lalonde had taken me aside and told me how that happened to most girls who swam, and that if I fine-tuned my technique, I'd make up the time. She'd also encouraged me to switch my specialty from breaststroke to crawl. "Focus on a different stroke," she'd told me. "Let go and move forward."

I listened, since when it comes to swimming, Madame Lalonde knows her stuff. "Don't dive quite so deep. If you're closer to the surface, you'll lose less time coming up for air," she'd told me after Saturday practice. I can't wait to try that out.

With the provincials coming up, Madame Lalonde wanted us to build our endurance, which explained why she was making us run. In a race — especially a long one — swimmers have to be able to go the distance.

"Are you sure you don't want me to walk with you?" I asked Ashley.

"Go on."

Just then, Svetlana came jogging up from behind. "Do you need company?" she asked Ashley, sounding concerned.

I took that as my cue to move on. I was glad Svetlana was alone. Matt-less. Matt-free. Minus Matt.

Matt. Every time my running shoes touched the gravel, his name popped into my head. I could see he wasn't up ahead, but I wouldn't let myself turn around to look for him.

I was happy to know he wasn't jogging with you-know-who. I hoped Ashley was right about Matt's not liking Svetlana.

Matt was in my dream last night. It was coming back to me now, the way dreams do, when you aren't even trying to remember them.

I was crouched down on the starting block, ready to dive. I had my lucky bathing cap on — the white nylon one my mom gave me two birthdays ago. She used it to wrap my main gift, which was a diving watch. Instead of ribbon, she'd tied the whole thing up with a thick piece of red and white nylon cord — the kind they use in the pool to separate lanes. Mom used to do stuff like that before she got the navy blues.

In my dream, Matt was up in the lifeguard's chair, watching me. My lower legs were shaking like always before a race. I looked out at the water about two metres in front of me — that, I told myself, is where I want to be when I surface. And I won't let myself go in too deep. I pictured the dive — strong, but graceful, my tailbone rising into the air.

Then I imagined my arms moving into a crawl and my legs kicking out behind me. I could practically feel the water lapping against my skin.

At that moment, I realized I hadn't seen the girls I was up against. Why hadn't I checked them out on the starting blocks? Why hadn't I studied the race sheets posted on the bulletin board? I didn't even know their times.

I turned to check out the competition. Ashley was in the next lane. She lifted a finger from the bottom of the block and waved it at me. I felt my spine relax.

Suddenly, I noticed another swimmer I hadn't seen before. Her head was turned away, but something was familiar about her — the way she tapped her right toe as she waited on the starting block, and the curve of her thighs.

When she turned around, I was so surprised I nearly fell off the starting block. Mom! I recognized her high cheekbones and dark eyes. Only this was Mom the way she used to be — before I even knew her — when she was my age.

I must've groaned in my sleep, because when I woke up, Mom was leaning over the side of my bed. "What is it, baby?" she asked. Her eyes shone in the dark.

I hate when she calls me baby. I groaned some more so she'd think I was still asleep. When she reached over to stroke my forehead, I used my elbow to push her away. The flicker of hurt I saw in her eyes made me push even harder.

5

Running Late

I knew I should've walked.

If I'd walked, I'd be in the locker room by now — not standing at the 161 bus stop on a Tuesday morning feeling like an idiot.

It's eight blocks from my house to the pool; each block takes me about two-and-a-half minutes, which meant I was 20 minutes away. Most people don't know that being on a swim team improves your math. Ask me to divide anything by 25 — the Côte-des-Neiges pool is 25 metres long — and I can come up with the answer quicker than a calculator. Most of us do pretty well in math, especially on quizzes.

Even if I started walking now, I'd be late for practice. Or even worse, the bus might pass me on the way.

I'd turned off my alarm at 5:30 a.m., using the snooze button so I could get another 15 minutes of sleep. But my present situation had nothing to do with that. No, it was Mom's fault. If she'd driven me like she used to, I'd be on time. I imagined her lying in bed or walking downstairs in her bathrobe. Let's be honest, it isn't like she has a lot of other important stuff to do.

I looked down Van Horne Avenue, hoping to spot the yellow headlights of a city bus. At this time of day, traffic was light — mostly trucks crossing town on their way to the expressway.

Just then, a rusty car screeched to a halt in front of the bus shelter. The back door swung open, making a creaking sound. I stepped back. I wasn't about to get in some stranger's car. Even from where I was standing, I could smell the harsh scent of ammonia coming from inside the car.

"Do you vant a lift?" someone called out from the passenger seat. That accent could only belong to one person — Svetlana.

I nearly said no. But when I pictured Madame Lalonde wagging her finger at me and saying, "If you all slept in the way Victoria did today, we might as well kiss the provincials goodbye," I reconsidered.

Climbing into the backseat was a challenge — crossing over Svetlana's gym bag and a mountain of plastic pails loaded with sponges and cleaning products. I had to be careful not to hit my head on a tired-looking mop jutting out from a red pail.

Svetlana grinned as she reached over to grab her gym bag. At least now there was room for my feet.

"Thanks for stopping," I muttered. "I missed the bus…" I was about to explain how Mom usually drove me, but instead I let my voice trail off.

"Mama, dis is Vicky," Svetlana said. "Vicky — dis is my mama."

"Nice to meet you," the woman said. Though I'd seen most of the other kids' parents at practices or competitions, I'd never seen either of Svetlana's parents. Not that I'd ever given them much thought before. Maybe they worked odd hours.

Svetlana's mother didn't turn around to look at me until we reached the first stoplight. When she did, I noticed that her hair was the same pale blonde as Svetlana's, and cut short. Her tank top revealed strong shoulders — swimmer's shoulders.

"Svetlana," her mother said, after the light changed, "I vant

you to concentrate on your fingers — use zem to propel you
through the water."

"Yes, mama," Svetlana said, rolling her eyes in my direction.

"I used to svim," Svetlana's mother explained. Although her
eyes were on the road, I knew she was talking to me. "I vas on
the Russian national svim team," she added.

"Wow!" I said. That was impressive.

"Now is Svetlana's chance," her mother said as she pulled
into the parking lot.

"Thank you very much, Mrs.—"

"Slemko, our last name is Slemko," Svetlana said, helping
me out.

"Mrs. Slemko," I said.

As I got out of the car, I noticed white block letters on the
driver's side window that spelled: "KIEV CLEANING SER-
VICE." I knew Svetlana was born in the city of Kiev. Now I
understood the pails and mop. As Mrs. Slemko lifted her hand
to wave good-bye, I noticed her skin was cracked and dry —
maybe from cleaning products.

Usually, when Svetlana was around, I just felt irritated or
angry. Now, for the first time, I felt a little sorry for her and her
family.

But that feeling didn't last long. It disappeared when Svetlana slung her gym bag over her shoulder and announced, "I
invited Matt to come with me to zee bowling party on Friday."

6

Endurance Training

It must've been my morning for signs.

On a sheet of lined paper taped to the locker room door, I recognized Madame Lalonde's bold block letters saying: "NO BATHING SUITS TODAY."

I whipped my arms across my chest. "No way!" I said to Ashley, who was standing next to me, "We're swimming naked? Madame Lalonde wants us to get us in touch with our inner fish."

Ashley puckered her lips and made a gurgling sound like a fish. I laughed, even though I'd seen her fish imitation before. "It's not that bad," Ashley said, pointing to the small print at the bottom of the sign.

"Wear your shorts and T-shirt to the pool. Signed, Madame Lalonde," I said, reading the rest of the message out loud. "What is she thinking?" Ashley shrugged.

At the start of the season, Madame Lalonde had told us to keep an extra T-shirt and pair of shorts in our lockers. Mine were rolled up on the floor, stuffed under a towel.

Usually, things are quiet in the locker room before morning practice, but today, everyone was buzzing about the sign.

"Any bet Madame Lalonde is planning some torture for us? She's been pushing us hard lately," Denise observed.

"We need to work hard with the provincials coming up," Ashley said. "But I don't see what shorts and T-shirts have to do with it."

"Do you think zees T-shirt matches zees shorts?" asked Svetlana, smiling flirtatiously at her own reflection in the mirror.

I didn't say a thing. I wasn't about to give *her* fashion advice.

"You look fine," Ashley told her.

"You're sveet," Svetlana said, without turning away from the mirror.

"What about underwear? Madame Lalonde didn't say anything about underwear," Samra called out.

"Underwear is a given when you're wearing shorts and a T-shirt," I told her. "Ever notice how if you're invited to a party and it says wear something formal, they don't mention underwear. They just figure you'll have the sense to wear it."

"Good point," Samra said.

Personally, I was glad not to change into my swimsuit. I'd forgotten to take it out of my bag last night, so it was still wet from yesterday's practice. Nothing's more disgusting than putting on a clammy bathing suit. This, I decided, was also Mom's fault. In the old days, she'd have reminded me to hang it out the minute I got home from swimming.

The boys were already at the pool, waiting in their shorts and T-shirts. Matt was wearing a pair of loose-fitting khaki-coloured shorts that reached almost to his knees. He smiled in my direction. That cheered me up, till I realized Svetlana was behind me. Rats! I thought. Maybe he'd smiled at her.

Unfortunately, a smile isn't the sort of thing you can investigate. Excuse me, sir, did you just smile at me — or was that gorgeous smile directed at that annoying *witch* behind me — the one you're going bowling with Friday night?

Wouldn't it be fun to live in a world where you could say

what you really thought? The best part would be not having to keep so much inside. I think keeping stuff inside drives people crazy.

Clara did a quick head count to make sure we were all there. When Madame Lalonde walked out of her office she shouted, "Into the pool!"

No one moved. All eyes were on Madame Lalonde.

"What did you just say?" Juan asked. Of course, we were all wondering the same thing.

"Into the pool!" she repeated. "Now! Seven hundred and fifty metres of crawl!"

Matt and Juan were the first to dive in. Juan's shorts ballooned around his legs like sails when he hit the water. I looked down at my oversized white T-shirt and gym shorts, wishing there were less of them. Every ounce of fabric would add weight in the pool.

Of course, that was what Madame Lalonde wanted. Denise was right. This was another scheme for building our endurance. At least Madame Lalonde hadn't made us wear our socks and shoes.

My eyes met Ashley's. She was giving me this look that said we might as well get it over with. So we jumped into the next lane.

The others followed. I could hear the plopping sounds of their bodies hitting the water as the weight of my clothes dragged me towards the pool floor.

What an awful feeling — heavy, helpless and worst of all, slow. Usually, it takes me about seven seconds to surface after jumping in, but in clothes, it took way longer. Every part of me felt like I was moving in slow motion.

Up ahead in the next lane, I could see Matt's blurry outline. He and Juan had already started their laps.

Ashley and I surfaced together, sputtering for air. This time, we didn't exchange looks. That would have taken too much energy. Instead, we just started to swim, arms and legs heavier than usual, struggling to stay above water.

Thirty laps of this, I thought to myself, will take forever. But we had no choice except to start. I've had that feeling before. Like at school, during a math test when I'm trying to solve an equation. Sometimes, I imagine giving up — crumpling the question sheet into a ball, chucking it into the garbage pail and walking out of the classroom. Of course, I never do.

And then, just like that, you figure out what X stands for.

Only this time, there wasn't any X.

Unless you count the X in exercise.

You think about weird stuff like that when you're swimming.

Breathing was getting harder, but I forced myself to keep moving. I slogged through the water.

When I finally finished, Matt and Juan were stretching at the side of the pool.

"Hey, Victoria!" Juan called out as I reached the ledge. "Wanna go to the bowling party Friday night?"

I didn't know what to say — except yes.

7

Table for Two

"Your father's working late. Your mother's having a bath. There's spaghetti with tomato sauce on the stove," Abigail told me. She'd been about to lock the door behind her when she'd spotted me walking up the flagstone path to our house.

"Homemade?" I asked.

"Of course," Abigail said, thrusting out her chin. Cooking from scratch is a point of pride with Abigail. Nothing upsets her more than frozen pizza or tomato sauce from a jar.

"Yum," I said. Two practices with school in between sure builds an appetite.

"How's the swimming?" Abigail asked, reaching out to smooth a curl on my forehead. I'd known Abigail forever. She'd been my baby nurse, and about 30 years before that, she'd been my mom's baby nurse in Vancouver.

"Pretty good," I said. "Except this morning — Madame Lalonde made us swim in our clothes."

"In your clothes? Don't tell me you went to school in wet clothes!" Abigail said, making a tsk-ing sound at the end of her sentence.

"No, no. We had extra clothes. Except, uh, underwear," I explained. "The funny thing is this afternoon's practice went super well. We were all so glad to be back in swimsuits our times picked up."

"You mustn't push too hard," Abigail said. Though she was fumbling with her purse, trying to find her bus pass, I knew she was watching me.

"Don't worry," I said.

"I do worry," she said. "It's my nature. Keep an eye on your mother, okay?"

"How is she?" I asked. Between being late this morning, getting angry with Svetlana, swimming in my clothes and feeling weird about going to the bowling party with Juan, I hadn't thought about Mom. And that, I realized now, had been a relief.

"Still eating like a bird."

I almost smiled. With Abigail, everything came down to food. "Maybe she'll have spaghetti," I told her.

"Maybe," Abigail said, giving my hair a final rumple before she rushed off to catch her bus.

I threw my backpack and gym bag on the hallway floor. Note to self: Rinse out bathing suit and hang it to dry before going to bed.

The house was quiet except for the hum of the air conditioner. The front hallway leading to the living room was lined with portraits. Though I'd never met any of the people in those paintings, I felt I knew them. Distant relatives on Dad's side, they'd been watching me grow up from inside their fancy golden frames.

"What do you have to say for yourself?" I asked my favourite one — great-uncle Francis. He looked like my dad, except his hair was white and he had this big moustache that curled up at both ends like a pair of furry snails. "Nothing, as usual," I said, giving him a wink.

My mother was coming down the spiral staircase. She was wearing her long pink velour bathrobe, and her blonde curls were piled on top of her head like a crown. If her shoulders weren't slouched, she'd look almost regal.

"You're home," she said, sounding surprised.

Great, I thought. I've been getting home at 7:00 for the last four years.

"You hardly need me anymore," my mom whispered as she followed me into the kitchen.

I was tempted to pretend I hadn't heard her. "Of course I do," I said. But inside, I couldn't help thinking that in a way, she was right. Who needs a mom who lies around all day and makes bizarre remarks?

The kitchen smelled of garlic and tomatoes. Abigail had set the table for two and left us a tossed salad. All I had to do was warm up the spaghetti. "We had two practices today," I said as I turned on the burner.

"Right," my mom said, "it's Tuesday, isn't it?"

"Yup, Tuesday," I said, my back turned to her. Welcome to planet Earth, I thought. The pot made a sizzling sound.

I felt her eyes on me as I used a wooden spoon to stir the spaghetti. "You're getting so grown up," she said. She made it sound like a bad thing.

I tried to say something that might make her feel better. "I'm not that grown up," I told her. "I'm only 13."

"Nearly 14," she said as if that was bad enough. "You're changing."

I looked down at my chest and hips. Mom was right. I was changing. Growing up — sometimes it did feel kinda weird. But I didn't want to talk about it. "Spaghetti looks good," I said as I brought the pan over to where Mom was sitting.

She loosened her napkin from the napkin ring and sighed.

I dished a small helping of noodles onto her plate.

"I'm not very hungry," she whispered. As if I couldn't figure that out.

I loaded my own plate with noodles. "Should we leave some for Dad?" I asked.

"I don't know," she said.

I sprinkled Parmesan cheese over my spaghetti. Mom covered her plate with her hands to show me she didn't want cheese. "I had a big lunch," she whispered.

"You did?" I was surprised. "Did you go out?"

"No," she said, avoiding my eyes. "I was in all day."

"Mom," I said, "What's going on?"

She didn't answer my question. When she looked at me, her eyes looked sad — sad and empty. Looking at her made me feel sad and empty, too. "I don't know, Victoria. I just don't know," she said.

Just then, I felt a drop of warm water land on the tip of my nose. It wasn't a tear. If I'd been outside, I'd have thought it was rain. "That's funny," I said, wiping the water with the back of my hand.

"What?" Mom asked, her voice sounding stronger. She seemed glad we'd switched subjects.

"It's raining in here," I said as I felt a few more drops of water.

"Raining inside? My goodness, I just felt a drop, too," my mother said, giggling as she used her napkin to dab at the wet spot on her cheek.

It was nice to hear her laugh. I leaned back in my chair and looked up at the ceiling. That's when I noticed a round, damp spot the size of a baseball. The water had to be coming from my parents' bathroom, which was directly upstairs.

"Mom!" I said. "Is a pipe leaking or something?"

"Oh my, I think I forgot to turn off the bath water," Mom said, covering her face with her hands. "I don't know what's wrong with me. I just don't know." The hum of the air conditioner must have blocked out the sound of running water. I had a feeling Mom needed a hug. But I knew I had to run upstairs to turn off the faucet before the flooding got any worse. Later, I'd break it to Dad that we'd probably need to call someone to fix the ceiling.

I knew something else, too — that when I'd finished drying off the bathroom floor and got back downstairs, my mom would still be sitting at the table. And her hands would still be over her face.

8

Some Party!

Yes!" Svetlana called out as she watched her bowling ball slam into the pins. A perfect strike. Don't tell me her dad had been a member of the Russian bowling team.

"Fantastique!" Denise shouted, jumping up from her seat. Her half-eaten bag of Tostitos dropped to the ground.

Some cartoon figures danced on the overhead screen.

We were playing cross lanes, girls against boys, which meant our teams were alternating between two lanes.

Madame Lalonde and Clara were sitting in the nearby nest of seats, sipping coffee and watching us. Clara clapped when Samra knocked two pins down after her second turn. "You're getting the hang of it," Clara called out when Samra passed her.

Getting the hang of it? She had to be kidding.

"Do you really think so?" Samra asked. And of course, Clara said she really did.

Juan was up next. He turned towards me as he slid his fingers into the bowling ball. I could tell he wanted to make sure I was watching him.

Nothing's wrong with Juan. Sure, he was a bit skinny and his shoulders sloped inwards like a lot of swimmers' shoulders do, but he was tall and sort of good-looking. There was just one problem. He wasn't Matt.

Juan knocked down eight pins. "Good work, man," Matt congratulated Juan as he headed back to his seat. Juan laughed and flexed his biceps. "I'm tough," he said, looking at me again. This time, I pretended not to notice.

Boy, was I miserable. I refused to cheer for Svetlana, even though we were on the same side. I couldn't cheer for Juan either. I didn't want him to think I liked him — not in that way.

All I wanted to cheer for was the end of this dumb party.

I should never have said yes when Juan asked me to go with him. At least, I hadn't let him pick me up at my house. "Don't go out of your way to get me," I'd told him when I spotted him waiting outside the complex after this afternoon's practice, "Ashley and I will meet you at Paré at 7:30." Paré Lanes, the bowling alley, was only a ten-minute drive from the sports complex.

It was all Svetlana's fault. We'd had lots of swim team parties before, but this was the first time anyone had come in pairs. I had a feeling Juan only invited me after he found out Matt was going with Svetlana. Of course, that was also why I'd said yes to Juan. Talk about peer pressure.

"Nobody invited me," Ashley had complained on the way to the bowling alley. Her dad had given us a ride and was picking us up at 10:00.

"I invited you," I said, squeezing her hand.

"No you didn't. You're going with Juan."

"Really? Look around this car. Who would you say I was going with? Besides, you can have Juan."

"I don't want him — and neither do you," Ashley said, which had made us both laugh.

Now Ashley was nudging my elbow. "Hurry up, Vic. You're up."

I dragged myself up from my seat. Who cares about bowling,

anyhow? But something changed when I eyed the pins at the far end. Or maybe it was the clanging sound of them being re-set. Whatever it was, I started feeling as though I cared about bowling.

I sent the ball rolling down the lane. It headed down the center, but then veered off course and into the gutter. I took a couple of seconds to concentrate before my next try. This time, I pictured the bowling ball picking up speed, rolling down the lane and knocking over all ten pins. That's exactly what it did.

"Nice job!" the girls shouted. Clara nodded in my direction as she got up from her seat. I figured she wanted another coffee.

Matt took his turn at the next lane. "Nice spare," he whispered to me, as he stretched his arm out behind him.

"Thanks," I muttered.

I knew what would happen next. Matt would take his turn and no matter how he bowled, Svetlana would cheer for him — loudly. I could practically hear her yell, "Vay to go! Nice work, Barracuda!" Rather than stick around to see my prediction come true, I decided to take a bathroom break. At least there, I'd be spared Svetlana's performance.

Clara wasn't at the concession counter. She was leaving one of the bathroom stalls when I walked in. She smiled at me, but she didn't mention my spare. "Having fun?" she asked as she walked towards the row of sinks.

"Yeah — I'm getting into it."

"Uh-huh," Clara said, turning on the water. "Good!"

"Did you catch my spare?"

"Uh-huh," she said again.

"How come you got so excited when Samra knocked over two pins — and you don't say anything when one of us gets a spare or a strike?"

"Samra needs someone to root for her," Clara said. "Kids like you and Svetlana—" (I couldn't help wincing when she mentioned us in the same sentence) "are used to people rooting for you."

Maybe she had a point. "Well," I told her, "I could still use someone cheering for me."

"You seem to be bowling just fine," Clara said.

"It's not bowling," I muttered. "It's other stuff."

"Other stuff?" Clara seemed interested.

"Yeah, like life. Like Svetlana." I hadn't meant to tell her, but the words just spilled out.

"I see," Clara said, but I didn't get the feeling she really did.

"She's after Matt."

"Really? I thought he liked you."

"You did?" I asked.

"Absolutely," Clara said as she finished washing her hands. "I've noticed how you try to swim behind him during practices …" (I felt my cheeks get hot when she said that.) "… and how he looks up at the deck until you get there and picks up his pace when you're swimming behind him. He's been trying to impress you."

"Really?" I was starting to feel better.

"Really."

"Svetlana invited him to the party tonight," I told Clara.

"What are you going to do?" she asked.

"Do?" I asked. "Nothing. Except feel lousy, I guess."

"That doesn't sound like much of a plan," Clara said, drying her hands. She patted my shoulder on her way out the bathroom. "Something tells me you can do better than that."

9

Change of Plans

Plan, shplan.

I don't believe in plans. Well, that's not exactly true. I believe in plans when it comes to sports. You need a plan if you want to improve your time in the pool. But I don't believe in people plans.

That's not exactly true, either. What I mean is I don't believe in other-people-plans. You can make a plan for yourself to study harder or be nicer to somebody, but other people have to make their own plans.

If Matt liked Svetlana, that just meant he had bad taste. I can't do anything about that. If he didn't like her, he should have said no when she invited him to the bowling party.

Not that I was an expert in saying no. Look at me — I said yes to Juan.

If I were going to come up with a plan, it wouldn't be to try to make Matt like me more, or even to double-cross Svetlana (though that idea was tempting). No, all I could do was straighten things out with Juan, before things got more complicated.

When I walked back to our lanes, Juan was gesturing towards the empty seat next to his. "I kept it for you," he said.

"Lucky you," Ashley whispered as I squeezed past her.

I could tell from the scoreboard that Matt had knocked over seven more pins and Svetlana had got another strike. So far, the girls were winning.

Denise was up.

"Let's go!" I called out along with the other girls.

Juan was about to take his turn in the next lane.

Denise leaned her body over to one side as the bowling ball veered in the same direction, and then off course. Then she leaned over in the other direction, as if, from where she was standing, she could control the bowling ball. "Ah, non!" she cried out, stomping her foot when the ball dropped into the gutter.

I was relieved when Juan didn't stop to check if I was watching him. "Go, Juan, go!" the boys called out as Juan hurled the ball down the lane.

"No, Juan, no!" the girls yelled. This time, I didn't join in. I may not have liked Juan in that way I was talking about, but I did feel a certain loyalty towards him. After all, he had invited me to the party — even though I shouldn't have said yes. Feelings, I thought, can get pretty complicated sometimes.

First Juan's bowling ball struck the center pin, then the other pins tumbled over in a messy heap. Juan raised his arms into the air. "Go, Juan, go!" he said, laughing.

Our voices were hoarse from shouting. One thing about bowling is that — unlike in the pool — you get to make noise. People need to be loud sometimes. And when you're in a bowling alley, regular sounds seem even noisier because of the echo. It's like being in a cave.

Madame Lalonde covered her ears. "Take you kids out of the pool, and you go nuts." She turned to Clara. "But then they swim better afterwards."

"Way to go!" I told Juan when he sat back down. I had to say something — and it had been a nice strike.

"Which team are you rooting for?" Juan asked, grinning.

"My own, of course," I said, looking over at the other girls.

That's when I felt Juan slip his arm behind my back. Uh-oh! I thought, as I did my best to inch forward. I looked over at Ashley — thinking she'd be watching — but she had just stood up to take her turn.

"Go, Ashley!" I yelled, jumping up from my seat and untangling myself from Juan's arm. "Fantastic!" I yelled again when she knocked over eight pins.

"Juan," I said, when I finally stopped cheering and sat down, making sure to leave no room for his arm. "Wanna get some popcorn?"

"Sure," he said, popping up from his seat like a jack-in-the-box.

"Listen, Juan, I need to tell you something," I began as we approached the snack bar.

"What's that?" he asked. I was so busy watching his arms — hoping he wouldn't slip one of them around me again — that I couldn't concentrate.

"Juan, what I want to tell you is," I began, stumbling over my words, "is, is that I'm too young to go on dates." Phew, I finally got that out! It wasn't exactly true, but I couldn't tell him I liked somebody else.

"Is that you or your parents talking?" Juan wanted to know.

"Me," I said. "Not my parents. I'm too young to go out with guys," I said, more loudly this time.

"You're too young to go out with guys," a voice repeated. For a second, I was confused. I knew it wasn't Juan.

When I turned to see who had joined in on our conversation, I felt my stomach lurch. Matt was there, leaning over the counter. When our eyes met, he gave me that smile of his. "Two Cokes, please," he called out to the woman behind the counter.

There wasn't time to feel embarrassed. Just then, someone came rushing into the bowling alley. They hadn't bothered to park their car; they'd left it right by the front door, without even turning off the headlights.

I recognized the small black sports car. What's my dad doing here?

He must've spotted me right away because he rushed over to where I was standing between the two boys. "Dad," I said, "this is—"

But I never got to introduce him to Juan or Matt. Dad grabbed my wrist and marched me towards the door. "What are you doing out so late, anyhow?" he asked, as if I'd done something wrong.

"It's only nine-thirty," I said, wondering why he was going nuts. Did he think I was still ten? "We're having a team party, Dad. We have them all the time," I tried to explain as I rushed to keep up with him. "Abigail knew about it. So did Mom."

He slowed down for a second when I mentioned Mom.

But he didn't say another word till we were inside the car. "This is about your mom," he said. "She's gone."

10

Upside Down

Swimming helped.

Even though I was really tired — I couldn't sleep last night after Dad broke the news — the repetitive movement of my arms and legs felt soothing. So did being in water. Some people say swimming represents a kind of return to the womb — to a time when we had no worries, and when we were perfectly connected to our mothers.

Only now, I had nothing but worries. As for my connection to my mom, let's just say that at the moment, it was pretty much non-existent. Sure I had a mother, but where was she?

Dad thought I might know, which was why he'd shown up at the bowling alley. Mom had left her car, but her clothes, make-up and even her suitcase were missing. "Did she mention any plans?" he'd asked on the way home. "Was there any place she said she wanted to visit?"

I'd felt like asking him where he'd been the last two months. Hadn't he noticed that Mom didn't go anywhere? That she spent most of her time lying in bed with a washcloth on her head? Did he really think Mom had suddenly been bitten by the travel bug? That she was off on a cruise or better yet, some jungle safari?

"Nope," I'd told him, "she didn't say anything — only that

she didn't know what was wrong with her."

Dad had winced when I said that. Then his cell phone rang. "William Miller here," he said, picking it up.

I heard a muffled voice say something about a broken water main.

"I'm with my daughter," my dad said, catching my eye. "I'll phone you back."

My dad didn't usually get off the phone on my account.

"Does Abigail know?" I asked.

"I phoned her as soon as I realized Mom was missing. Like you, she doesn't have any idea where she might be. I also tried Aunt Jody, and some of Mom's friends. They haven't heard from her in months."

"Dad," I'd said, laying my hand on his wrist and sounding calmer than I felt, "we should call the police."

"No," he protested, slipping his wrist out from under my hand and gripping the steering wheel with both hands. His knuckles were so white they practically glowed in the dark. "Not yet. I don't want them involved. Next thing we know, this'll be all over the newspapers and TV. Tess Miller, wife of prominent realtor, disappears into thin air," he said, waving one hand into the air, as if that was really where Mom had gone. "No, your mom and I have had enough trouble with the media," he muttered to himself.

I wondered what he meant by that. I'm the kind of person who doesn't usually know what to say on the spot. But now that I was swimming, I knew exactly what I should have said. Dad, I should have begun, this isn't all about you. Mom's not just some "wife of." Who cares how prominent you are and whether Mom's disappearance makes the news? What matters is that we find her — and make sure she's okay.

What I just thought about her being okay made me nervous. What if Mom did something really crazy — like tried to hurt herself? But my mind couldn't go there. Mom had better be all right, I thought.

I was having trouble focusing on Madame Lalonde's instructions. Though she was standing at the edge of the pool, her voice seemed to be coming from far away. "Stay in your tuck longer, Victoria," I heard her say as I began another lap of crawl. "That will give more power for your push-offs."

I nodded. But I wasn't sure that by the time I reached the other end of the pool, I'd remember what Madame Lalonde had said.

When I came up to breathe, I peeked up at the stands. A small group of parents was huddled together, watching our practice. For a second, I thought I saw my mom. She was sitting in the middle of the front row, holding a washcloth to her forehead. I gulped for air. When I looked again, she was gone.

"Let's go team!" I could hear Madame Lalonde shout. "District finals are one week from today. You'll have to do way better than this!"

The other kids started to pick up speed. A whir of energy filled the pool — more ripples, more kicking, more movement. No matter how tired I was, I scooped more deeply with my hands and kicked harder. I could see the pink soles of Matt's feet just up ahead of me.

Funny, I thought, I hadn't even thought of Matt today. Problems, I decided, are like waves. When a bigger, scarier-looking one comes along – *whoosh!* — you forget about the last one.

I looked up at the stands again. No sign of Mom. For a second, I let myself imagine what life would be like if she never came back. That heavy feeling I get when I walk into the house and she's just sitting there, looking sad, would be gone for good.

But I felt that heavy feeling now as I struggled to move faster in the water.

"Much better!" Madame Lalonde said when practice was finally over and we climbed out of the pool. "Before you leave today," she said, as she followed us to the locker rooms, "check the bulletin board outside. I've posted your projected times for next week's competition."

Svetlana ran out to the hallway without bothering to change into her regular clothes. "Victoria," she said, when she returned to the locker room. "You're only two seconds behind me." She waved two fingers in my face. "Do you really zink you can beat me?"

"To tell you the truth, Svetlana," I told her, "I'm not sure I'll be competing in the district finals."

I figured that would make Svetlana's day. We both knew I was her only real competition on our team. If I wasn't there, she'd only have to worry about the strong swimmers on the other Montreal teams. Instead, a long shadow crossed over Svetlana's face, leaving no sign of her usual grin.

"You can't do zat," she said.

"Wanna bet?"

11

"Trust Me"

Dad was sitting in the blue velvet armchair in the downstairs den.

He never sits there.

Usually, he's in his office, sitting in his leather chair — feet stretched out in front of him — talking on the phone, of course.

Dad had covered his face with his hands, but he dropped them to his knees when he heard me come in. Geez, I thought, next thing I know he'll be walking around with a washcloth on his head.

He tapped the arm of the chair, and I sat down on it. We hadn't sat so close in a while. I know this sounds weird, but sometimes I think Dad's a bit afraid of me. Then he reached out and stroked my hair the way he used to when I was little, and I got this tight feeling in my throat.

"How ya doin'?" he asked in a low voice.

"I'm okay. You?"

"I'm okay," he said gently, but we both knew we weren't. "I was thinking, Victoria," he continued, "you don't have to go to practice this week if you don't want to."

"Okay." Then after a couple of seconds, I added, "I'm kind of used to going."

"If it's good for you," he said, looking as if he didn't quite know what to make of me, "then by all means, go."

"I'm just not sure I want to compete next weekend," I told him.

"What's next weekend?"

"The district finals. After that, it's the provincials in June."

"I see," he said. I noticed he was drumming his fingers on his knee. "I take it you have to compete this weekend to qualify for the provincials."

"Right," I said, half expecting him to talk me into racing.

But he didn't. He just nodded.

For a few seconds, neither of us said a word.

"Do you remember the day you learned to swim?"

That was a surprising question, coming from him. "Mostly I remember the feeling," I replied.

"I was holding you in the shallow end of the pool."

"You were talking with some other dad. About money." I didn't mean to sound accusing, but that's how it came out.

"Money?" Dad seemed surprised.

"Yup, you were talking about investments."

"Tell me about the feeling," he said.

"I knew I was floating when I stopped feeling your hands. At first I was scared, but mostly excited. It felt like flying — only in the water. I wanted to tell you, but I knew if I did, the feeling would end. Then someone yelled so loud it echoed underwater. That was Mom, right?"

Dad started twisting his wedding ring round and round his finger. I could tell he was thinking back. "She was furious with me," he said. "She came rushing to the side of the pool. 'Don't let go of her, Bill!'" he shrieked, imitating my mom's worried voice.

"Why was she so upset?" I asked.

"That's just Mom." Then, just like that, Dad's face went

blank, as if a curtain had been drawn over it.

At least now we were talking about her. "Dad, I really think we should call the police. She's been gone three days."

"We'll give it a little longer. I'm convinced she'll be home soon," he said, without looking up. But his voice sounded tense and he was still fiddling with his wedding ring.

I hoped he was right. But if you ask me, waiting around didn't seem to be working. Mom hadn't phoned or sent a message. Imagine how freaked out they'd be if I pulled something like that.

"But Dad," I said, "what if Mom—"

He didn't let me finish my sentence. "Your mom'll be fine," he insisted. "Trust me. She's done this kind of thing befo—" Dad gulped, as if he'd said too much.

"She has? When?" I could remember Mom having the blues, but I couldn't remember her ever being away, except when she and Dad were on vacation.

"She wouldn't want me to talk about it. Besides it happened before you were born. The main thing is — she always came back."

"But Dad—" I tried again.

"No buts, Victoria."

There was a knock at the door.

"Mr. Miller …" Abigail had agreed to work late a few evenings since Mom's disappearance. "Would you like some tea?"

"That would be lovely, Abigail."

"What about you, dear?" Abigail asked, looking over at me.

"Na," I said. "But thanks."

Then my dad crossed his legs and reached for some business magazine on the coffee table. That meant the conversation was over.

* * *

Not knowing what else to do with myself after school the next afternoon, I went to practice. Like I told Dad, I was used to it. Another good thing about practice is that it's exhausting. If it weren't for swimming, I wouldn't have gotten much sleep over the last few days.

Though I knew it didn't make sense, I couldn't stop looking for Mom — on the bus (not that she ever took the bus) in the stands during practice, not that she'd come to practice since the fall, even in the hallway at school.

"What's this I hear about you not competing this weekend?" Madame Lalonde asked when I finished my laps. Clara was standing behind her, making no attempt to hide the fact she was listening in.

I figured Svetlana must've talked to Madame Lalonde. "I should've told you," I said, looking down at my feet. The skin on my toes was shriveled from having been in the water so long.

"What's the matter, Victoria?" Madame Lalonde wanted to know.

"It's personal stuff. If you don't mind, I'd rather not discuss it," I said. It was hard to say, but I felt better once the words were out.

Madame Lalonde took two steps back, as if she didn't want to crowd me. "I respect that," she said. "But I want to tell you something. Whenever I had trouble in my life — and believe me, you're not the only kid who's ever had it rough — swimming helped. So did competing. The pool was one place where I could control things. You let me know if you want to talk about it," she said.

Without waiting for me to respond, Madame Lalonde turned and walked towards her office.

That left Clara and me alone at the side of the pool.

"Guy trouble?" she asked.

"*Mom* trouble," I said.

"Anything I can do to help?"

"Like I said, I don't want to talk about it. I can't talk about it." Then, without planning it, more words came gushing out — like water from a burst water main. "She took off," I said, "four days ago. My dad won't call the police. He says she's done it before and she'll be back soon, but he's mostly worried about it getting into the newspapers."

Of course, if my dad didn't want to go the police, he probably wouldn't want me discussing all this with someone I hardly knew. "You won't tell anyone, will you?"

"Of course not," Clara said, her eyes meeting mine.

"Not even Madame Lalonde."

"Not even Madame Lalonde," Clara agreed.

I couldn't deny it was a relief to tell someone what was going on. Besides, I thought, Clara's writing that thesis thing for university, so she probably knows a lot about doing research. "If it were you," I asked, "How would you try to track down a missing person?"

I could tell from the lines on her forehead that Clara was thinking. "Hmm," she said at last, "I'd start by asking 'Why?' I'd try to figure out what would make someone like your mom want to disappear."

"I don't have a clue why," I said.

"Well then, that's the first thing you'll have to find out."

12

The Investigation Begins

Okay, Abigail's nearly at the bus stop," Ashley whispered. She was crouched in front of the window in my parents' bedroom. With her body covered by the white gauzy curtains, she looked like a ghost.

Whispering wasn't necessary, seeing as we were the only two people in the house. We'd waited for Abigail to leave. She'd be furious if she found us rifling through Mom's drawers. I could imagine her scolding me the way she used to when she caught me raiding the cookie jar. Could I help it if she made such good cookies?

My parents' bedroom felt empty. Actually, since Mom's disappearance, the whole house felt empty. Sure, the air conditioner was still humming, and my distant relatives were still staring out from their golden frames downstairs. But everything felt hollow — blank.

My parents' bed was perfectly made, the corners tucked in by Abigail, the pillows fluffed the way Mom liked them. The only sign Dad had slept here last night was the small leather tray by his side of the bed where he kept his change.

I was glad I'd told Ashley about my mom. "All moms need a break sometimes. It's only Tuesday. I'm sure she'll be back by the end of the week feeling way better than before she left,"

Ashley had said, looking sympathetic.

I'd also told Ashley what Clara had said about figuring out the "Why?" That's when Ashley came up with the idea of searching my parents' bedroom for clues.

"I thought you didn't like Clara. You're always saying how she pays too much attention to the slow swimmers," Ashley had said. "Now you're quoting her like she's Shakespeare."

"You're right," I said. "I didn't like her. But she's grown on me."

"Grown on you?" Ashley said, wagging her finger in the air. "Next thing you know Svetlana'll be growing on you."

"I don't think so," I said.

I took a deep breath as I tugged open the small drawer at the top of Mom's nightstand. Suddenly, the smell of lavender water — her fragrance — was everywhere. I don't think I really missed my mom till that moment. Sure, the house felt empty and I was worried about her, but it wasn't the same.

Now the sweet scent reminded me of the mom I used to have — the smiling mom who'd rush to the door when I came home and drop whatever she was doing to listen to my stories about school and swimming. I missed that mom so much it hurt.

A pile of linen handkerchiefs lay neatly folded at the front of the drawer. Behind them, was the pair of thick blue woolen socks my mom liked to wear around the house on winter nights. Even her socks smelled like lavender.

"Boy! She sure has a ton of clothes!" Ashley said. She was inside the walk-in closet at the other end of the room. I heard the sound of metal hangers clanging against each other as Ashley made her way into the back of the closet.

"Svetlana's upset about you not competing on Saturday," Ashley said in a loud voice so I'd be able to hear her from inside the closet.

"How come we're still talking about Svetlana?" I asked.

"Sorry," Ashley said, not sounding sorry at all. A moment later, she peeked her head out. "Did you really mean it about not competing this weekend?" she asked.

"I'm pretty upset, Ash."

Ashley plopped down next to me on the soft ivory-coloured carpet. That's one thing about Ashley. When you need her, she's there — without even asking her to come over. "Who cares about swimming, anyway?" she said, running her fingers over one of the woolen socks.

"That's right," I said, turning back to the drawer, which was now almost empty.

Next I pulled out a packet of greeting cards held together by a thick elastic band. The edges of the cards were yellow and frayed. When I tried to loosen the top card from the packet, the elastic band flew into the air, ricocheting off the wall and landing at Ashley's feet.

I flipped through the cards. Most were decorated with flowers; a couple had pictures of sunsets on them. Another had a pair of cats, sitting together on a fence, their tails touching. "Happy Anniversary to My Darling Wife. Happy Birthday Sweetheart. To the Love of My Life," I said, reading the covers of the cards out loud.

"Wow," Ashley said. "I bet my dad never sent those kinds of cards to my mom — even when they were still married."

"Who'd have guessed my dad was the romantic type?" I said, reaching for the elastic.

"They look old," Ashley said. "I guess she was saving them."

The cards were arranged by date. At the bottom of the pile was a flowery one, a first anniversary card. The card at the top was a birthday card. Even though I felt a little snoopy, I opened it. It was dated January 20, 2000. My mom's birthday four years ago.

"I wonder where she keeps the more recent cards," Ashley said.

"Maybe there aren't any," I said, thinking how busy Dad always was.

"What's this?" Ashley asked, lifting the pile of handkerchiefs from the carpet.

"Just handkerchiefs."

"No," said Ashley, "something's tucked in here. Look!"

Ashley was right. As she showed me the handkerchiefs, a small ring tumbled to the carpet.

I picked it up and rolled the gold band between my fingers. When I was little, my mom used to let me play with all her jewelry. I knew her necklaces, earrings, pins and rings as well as I knew my old stuffed animals and dolls. But I'd never seen this ring.

As I slipped it on, I noticed the inside felt rough. When I looked closely, I could see it was engraved with thin, spidery letters.

"What's it say?" Ashley wanted to know.

"I see two pairs of initials: T.B. — that's my mom, Tess. Before she married Dad, her last name was Bryant. Don't ask me who R.L. is."

"One thing's for sure. He isn't your dad," Ashley said.

"I figured that," I told her, rolling my eyes.

"Do you think he's her boyfriend?" Ashley whispered.

Ashley's dad had a girlfriend. Ashley used to tell me how before her parents got divorced, her dad would come home late, smelling of alcohol and cigarettes. He'd met the girlfriend in a club downtown.

I pictured Mom moping around in her velour housecoat, hair uncombed.

"I don't think so. But—" I could practically feel an idea

forming in my brain— "maybe she *used* to have one."

Just then, we heard the chiming sound of our doorbell. "Quick!" I told Ashley as I stuffed the socks, greeting cards and handkerchiefs back into the drawer. "Shut the closet!" After we were downstairs, I realized I was still holding the ring, so I tucked it into my front pocket.

I could see Abigail's face peering through the glass window of the front door. "I forgot my keys," she announced as she flew past us and into the kitchen.

I tried to look innocent, but it's hard to fool Abigail.

"I get the feeling you've been in my cookie jar," she said. "Shouldn't you at least wait until after supper?"

13

Flip Turn

The initials R.L. — and what they might stand for — kept swimming through my head during practice: Robert Lewis … Ron Lake … Russell London … Or maybe R.L. stood for something more French-sounding, like Réal Leduc.

But if R.L. was someone my mom knew before she'd met Dad, he wouldn't have a French name, since my mom would still have been living in Vancouver. Rex Little. Only Rex sounded more like a dog than a person…

"Have you changed your mind about competing this week-end?" Madame Lalonde asked when I was putting on my bathing cap.

"No, I haven't," I told her as I tucked in the last stray curls. "But I wanted to come to practice. I was thinking about what you said — that swimming helps. Besides, I don't know what else to do with myself."

"Spoken like a real swimmer," Clara said. She was standing nearby, writing up our practice on the blackboard by the side of the pool.

"Laps first. Clara's putting them on the board. We'll finish with a little competition," Madame Lalonde announced, giving me a wink.

While I was swimming, I tried to think about my flip turns —

improving my tucks so I'd have more power when I was pushing off the wall — but it was hard. My mind kept coming up with new R.L. combinations. Reginald Livingstone! Nah, too old-fashioned. Mom would never fall for some guy named Reginald.

Talk about flip turns, I thought, as I completed my second one. My life was doing a flip turn! Everything was upside down.

I reached and pulled as if somehow those movements could set things right side up again.

Come on, Mom, come home! If I thought it hard enough, might she be able, somehow, to hear me?

"Everyone ready for a little competition?" Madame Lalonde called out after we'd finished our laps. "I want two teams — boys against girls," she explained. "Boys up first. Four hundred metres of breaststroke. Ready, fellows? On your marks, get set—" She blew her whistle and the boys dove into the pool, splashing noisily as their bodies hit the water.

I wrapped my towel over my shoulders to join Ashley and the other girls on the deck. Matt was in the lead, but Juan wasn't far behind.

Svetlana was leaning over the side of the pool, her face nearly touching the water. "Go, Barracuda!" she yelled every time Matt lifted his head to breathe.

Svetlana was yelling so hard, her voice got hoarse. But even her raspy cheers seemed to work. Matt won, beating Juan by nearly three seconds.

Matt's skin glistened as he climbed out of the pool. When he lifted his goggles to the top of his head and smiled up at me, I felt like I might lose my balance.

I was about to congratulate him when Svetlana came barreling over and planted herself between us. "Barracuda," she said, in a voice that sounded like a cat purring, "I'm zo proud of you."

Then, just like that, she leaned over and wrapped her arms tightly around Matt's shoulders. She gave him the longest hug I'd ever seen — even longer than the ones people give at the airport, when they're meeting up with relatives.

What was she thinking?

Matt blushed. First his face, then his back and legs turned a blotchy red. "Uhm," I heard him mutter as he shuffled from foot to foot. But he didn't push Svetlana away the way I hoped he would. Then another thought occurred to me. Maybe Matt liked Svetlana.

I was disgusted. I was angry. And I was jealous.

That's when I decided to compete at the district finals, after all. So much for being too upset about Mom. Now, I was too upset to stay home. I wanted revenge. And the only place I could imagine getting it was in the pool.

14

R.L.

Venir — to come. Mourir — to die.

Tomorrow was our Friday French quiz and I was supposed to be studying irregular verbs. Only it was getting harder and harder to concentrate. Images of my mom kept popping into my head. I'd imagine her lying on the couch — or standing by the stove, making me oatmeal before my morning practice.

"Did you ever have a boyfriend before you met your husband?"

Abigail was at the sink, peeling sweet potatoes.

"Of course I had boyfriends. I was a very attractive girl," she said, tossing back her silver hair.

I smiled. How clever of me not to begin asking questions straightaway about Mom. But Abigail wanted to tell me all about her old boyfriends. "One was an actor," she said, "charming, but unreliable. Another was a pilot. Much older than me and terribly wealthy. But when I met Charles (Charles was Abigail's husband), I forgot *all* the rest. One day, it'll happen to you too."

I wasn't convinced that Abigail had really forgotten all the rest. Not with the way she threw her head back and smiled when she talked about them.

"You haven't fallen in love, have you?" she asked, setting the potato peeler down on the counter.

Instead of answering her question, I asked another one. "What about Mom? Did she have other boyfriends besides Dad?"

"No," Abigail said, reaching for another sweet potato, "never."

"Not even one?"

"It's not my place to tell."

Ahh, I thought, now we're getting somewhere. "Come on," I said, coaxing her. And then I played my trump card. "It's not like Mom's around to tell me."

Abigail put down the potato peeler again and gave me a pained look. "Well," she said, "there were one or two fellows before she met your father. A young man named Lloyd when she was in high school. Then just before she got together with your father, there was someone — he was wild about her — Rupert, yes—"

Rupert? My mom went out with a guy named Rupert? But whatever I thought of his name, it began with an R.

"Rupert Linkletter. He'd have moved the Earth for your mother."

*   *   *

I googled him. It's not hard. Especially with a name like Rupert Linkletter. I mean, how many can there be? I typed Rupert Linkletter + Vancouver into the computer and a second later, his Web site popped up on my screen. Rupert Linkletter and Associates Plumbing. We can unblock any drain, fix any leak.

I couldn't help thinking that with the way my mom let the bathtub overflow, a plumber might come in handy.

I wrote to him without mentioning I was Mom's daughter. Otherwise, he might wonder why I didn't know where she was. Since he wouldn't be able to figure out my name from my e-mail address, which was winwinwin@yahoo.com, I decided to invent an alias for myself. I picked the name April, since I'd always liked it. The Briarwood part just came to me.

Here's what I wrote:

> *"Dear Rupert Linkletter, My name is April Briarwood and I am a journalist living in Montreal. I am working on a story about people who've moved from the West to the East coast. I am trying to track down Tess Bryant, someone I met when she first moved to Montreal.*
>
> *I believe you knew Tess when she lived in Vancouver. Are the two of you still in contact? If so, could you forward me her address? Please let me know as soon as possible. Yours truly, April Briarwood."*

I decided to change the "Yours truly" to "Best regards" since not everything I wrote in the e-mail was true. Then I checked for spelling mistakes — and sent it off. At least *now* I felt like I was doing something.

* * *

When I checked my e-mail half an hour later, he'd already written back. My hands trembled as I clicked on his message. If she'd kept that ring for so many years, might they still be in touch? Might she be there now, helping him unblock drains and fix leaks?

His reply was only a paragraph long:

> *"Hello April. Of course I remember Tess Bryant. It's hard to forget someone you had a crush on when you were growing up. But I haven't heard from her in years. We lost touch after the accident. If you do track her down —*

*and with an e-mail address like winwinwin, I have no
doubt you will — please say hello from me and ask her to
drop me a line if she gets a chance. Good luck with your
project. Rupert."*

They lost touch after the accident? What accident? So I wrote
back a one-sentence reply. "What accident do you mean?"

I checked my e-mail every ten minutes and then again in the
morning, but this time, Rupert Linkletter didn't write back.

* * *

I waited for Abigail to go grocery shopping so I could put the
ring with Rupert Linkletter's and my mom's initials back in her
nightstand. I tucked it back inside one of the handkerchiefs,
hoping Mom wouldn't notice when she came back. *If* she came
back ...

My mind wandered down that forbidden road again. What if
she had been in an accident? What if she'd hit her head and forgotten who she was? Or even worse, what if she'd overdosed on
sleeping pills or something? But then I pictured Mom lying in
bed with a washcloth on her head. The last thing she needed was
sleeping pills. That made me feel better, but still, when I looked
at my fingers, they were trembling.

The drawer got stuck when I tried to close it. At first, I thought
it was my fault because of the way my fingers kept shaking. So I
pushed harder, but that didn't help. Something was jammed back
there. When I reached inside, I felt a cardboard cylinder. When I
pried it loose, I realized it was a scrapbook.

Though I'd felt funny about going through Mom's cards, I
didn't feel funny about the scrapbook. After all, I figured, people keep stuff they're proud of in scrapbooks: prize ribbons,

awards, diplomas — that sort of thing. I wondered what my mom was most proud of. So I unrolled the book and opened it to the first page.

A photograph showed a girl wearing a swimsuit. For a second, I was startled. The girl in the photo looked just like me. But it was an old photo. I could tell because it was black and white with teeny triangles at the edges. Besides, I'd never owned a striped bathing suit. But the oval face and blonde curls were eerily familiar.

It was my mom.

I flipped the page. There were two more photos. A group of teenagers standing by the edge of a pool, smiling into the camera, arms interlocked. And in the second photo, my mom sitting in a lifeguard's chair, a whistle hanging from her neck. "She never told me she was a lifeguard," I said out loud.

When I turned to the next page, I began to understand why. An old newspaper clipping revealed a smaller version of that same photo of my mom in the lifeguard's chair. I gasped when I read the headline. "Six-year-old boy drowns at local pool."

So that was the accident Rupert Linkletter had been talking about.

15

Breaking News

Vancouver — A six-year-old boy drowned yesterday afternoon at Willow Pool in North Vancouver. Avery Munro fell into the deep end of the pool, and despite efforts by a lifeguard at the scene, the child was pronounced dead on arrival at the B.C. Children's Hospital.

Like many others trying to beat this week's heat wave, Munro's mother Gillian was spending the day at the pool with Avery and his siblings Michael, 8, and Amanda, 2.

"What happened is just tragic," said Patricia Kantor, a family friend who met with reporters last night. "Gillian lost sight of Avery when she went to the locker room to change the baby's diaper."

Because the pool was so crowded — officials estimate that some 500 people visited the pool yesterday — no one realized immediately that the child was in trouble. One witness, 10-year-old Lou-Anne Stafford, reported that she and her friends were not alarmed when they saw the boy tumble into the water. "We figured he could swim. And when he didn't come right up, we thought he was fooling around, holding his breath the way we do sometimes," said Lou-Anne.

Tess Bryant, the lifeguard on duty, noticed the boy under water, dove in, brought him to the deck and performed artificial respiration. She was unable to revive him. Neither could the ambulance technicians who arrived within minutes.

Avery had not had any formal swimming instruction.

Witnesses say that at the time of the incident, Bryant had been attempting to settle a dispute between two other youngsters.

Bryant, who was treated in hospital for shock after news of Munro's death, was unavailable for comment.

"Of course, what happened is too awful for words, but we have no plans to suspend Tess. This is her fifth summer working at Willow and she's one of our top lifeguards," said William Miller, who manages the pool.

An autopsy is scheduled for tomorrow. The funeral is expected to take place later this week.

* * *

My whole body shook as I read the story. Poor Avery, I thought. Poor Mom.

So Dad had managed the pool where she'd been a lifeguard. All they'd ever told me was they'd met at a party in Vancouver. They never said it was a pool party.

Just then, I looked at the date on which the story had been published: May 25, 1979. Avery Munro had drowned the day before — on May 24, 1979.

Today was May 30. Mom had been gone six days. She hadn't picked just any day to leave; she'd disappeared on the 24th — the 25th anniversary of that little boy's death.

No wonder spring was the hardest time of year for her.

No wonder she had trouble with things ending.

16

The District Competition

I'm glad you changed your mind about competing," Clara said when I passed her in the corridor outside the locker room on Saturday morning.

"How do you know I'm not just here to watch?" I said, spinning around to face her.

"Well, let's see," she said, looking me up and down, "you've got the pre-competition jitters: you're speaking quickly, your face is flushed. Plus — and this is the big giveaway, Victoria — you're carrying a gym bag."

I'd forgotten about the gym bag.

"How are things?" Clara asked, lowering her voice.

"A bit better," I said. "I'm starting to understand the why."

"Good. Now you'll have to figure out the where," she said. "And by the way, good luck in the pool."

"Thanks," I said as I swung open the door to the locker room, "for everything."

The locker room was as quiet as church before mass. All you could hear was the occasional thump of someone dropping a pair of shoes at the bottom of a locker, or the sounds of girls breathing — especially Ashley, who gets wheezy when she's nervous.

"Anyzing I can do to help?" Svetlana asked her.

"Want some water?" I joined in.

"No," Ashley said, clearing her throat and smiling at both of us. "I'm fine."

I'd worn my swimsuit underneath my street clothes, so all I had to do was slip out of my shorts and T-shirt.

Usually, the girls on our team spread out in the locker room, but today, because we were sharing space with girls from three other district teams, we stayed bunched together in one corner.

I recognized some girls from other competitions; and there were others I'd never seen before. I'll bet she's good at butterfly, I thought, noticing the strong shoulders on one girl. I turned away when she caught me watching her.

* * *

"Let's keep the lovey-dovey stuff out of it today," Madame Lalonde said at the end of her pre-race pep talk, looking right at Svetlana.

"I'll try," said Svetlana, grinning. You could tell she was enjoying the attention. If it were me, I'd have been totally embarrassed. On the other hand, if it were me, I'd never have hugged Matt in the first place. Not with everyone watching, anyway.

Matt just stared down at the tile floor of the deck. But I could see from the back of his neck that he was blushing again.

The younger kids were up first. Most people will tell you that watching swim meets is as bad as waiting in a doctor's office with nothing to read, but that's because they don't know what to look for. I watch everything — from the first dive into the water, to how the swimmers pace themselves, to how they make their turns and execute their strokes.

This morning was the qualifying heats. "Be sure to save some energy for later," Madame Lalonde warned us as we crowded round the long wooden table on the deck where she and Clara were sitting. Most of us had already checked the postings on the wall. If the other coaches had reported their swimmers' times accurately, several of us on the Côte-des-Neiges team stood a good chance of qualifying.

Though the district meet was being held at our pool, everything felt different today. The triangular flags that had been strung up over the pool fluttered in the air, and a noisy buzz filled the stands, which were jammed with parents. Most were sitting, but a few were leaning over the railing, trying to get a better view.

"Are your mom and dad here?" Matt asked, nudging me with his elbow.

"They couldn't make it," Ashley said, answering for me.

"What about your parents?" I asked Matt, steering the subject away from my family.

"They're sitting in the front row," he said pointing to a dark-haired couple. "My baby sister's here, too. See her? She's in my mom's lap."

Matt's mom must have noticed us looking up at them, because she lifted her daughter's hand and waved it in our direction. When we waved back, the little girl began to laugh — so loudly we could hear her from the deck.

"What's her name?" I asked.

"Flora," Matt told me.

"I love zat name," Svetlana said.

Because there were 10 lanes and we were grouped according to our times, I was in the same heat as Svetlana and Denise. So was the broad-shouldered girl I'd noticed downstairs. We started with the 100-metre breaststroke. When the buzzer sounded and it was our turn to dive in, I felt the hairs on my body prickle with excitement.

The hardest part was holding back. Remember what Madame Lalonde said, I told myself when I felt the urge to move more quickly through the water. Svetlana was two lanes over and I could see the outline of her body in the water. She was only slightly ahead of me. As for the broad-shouldered girl, she was swimming in one of the outside lanes — too far away for me to see her.

Just then, I couldn't help imagining Avery Munro's body as he sank to the bottom of that Vancouver pool 25 years ago. Stop it, I told myself. Just swim. But then I started picturing Svetlana hugging Matt, her body pressing up against his. Then I thought how my mom had been missing for over a week now. Next thing I knew, I was propelling myself through the water with a force I didn't know I had.

You go, girl! I thought to myself, when I realized I had managed to pass Svetlana. But by the time I reached the other end of the pool, I noticed a small crowd of swimmers and their coach. They were already gathered around the broad-shouldered girl, who'd come in first.

Svetlana touched the wall a second and a half after me, followed three seconds later by Denise.

"Nice work," said Madame Lalonde, who was waiting at the end of the pool. "The two of you will qualify," she said, nodding towards Sveltana and me. "But you've got more heats coming, so get some rest before you're up again."

Just then, I spotted a familiar-looking woman with pale blonde hair standing near the locker room door. She must've come down from the stands to watch us. I watched as she shaped one hand into a fist and pounded it against the wall. Hard.

Where had I seen her before?

Of course, I thought, she'd given me a ride that morning I was stranded at the bus stop. It was Mrs. Slemko — Svetlana's mother.

17

Trouble

I need quiet," Svetlana called out. She hadn't even turned around to see who it was when I walked into the locker room.

"No problem," I said.

She made a hmph-ing sound when she realized it was me, but then she went back to what she was doing. Whatever that was seemed to involve sitting cross-legged on a bench, breathing deeply through her nostrils and exhaling loudly through her mouth. Who did she think she was — Darth Vader?

As quietly as I could, I opened my locker, reached into my gym bag and took out the snack Abigail had packed. Two bottles of water, sliced apples, a couple of granola bars and a small baggie filled with cheddar cheese cubes.

"I'm visualizing my success," Svetlana announced, between breaths.

"I'm happy for you," I said, not knowing what else to say.

"My mama taught me how. She learned it in zee Ukraine."

"I saw your mom before," I said casually, as I tore open the foil wrapper of one of the granola bars. "She didn't seem happy."

"That's how she ees — never happy," Svetlana said, shrugging her shoulders. "I want zee best for you — only zee best!" she said in a high-pitched voice. It took me a couple of seconds to figure out she was imitating her mother.

"She stopped svimming because of problems with her shoulder. Now it's my turn to vin. Not just for me. For her, also," Svetlana said, using her finger to block one of her nostrils while breathing out of the other.

I took a bite of the granola bar. "So what exactly are you visualizing?" I asked.

"Do you really vant to know?" Svetlana asked.

"Yeah," I said, trying not to sound too interested. I had the feeling Svetlana was one of those people who, if they know you want something, suddenly don't want to let you have it.

"Vell," Svetlana said closing her eyes, "right now, I see myself doing zee 200-metre crawl. It's zee last lap. Zee water is full of waves. I see zee blue bottom of the pool and I smell chlorine. And oh, I see somezing else," she said in a faraway voice.

Without planning to, I closed my eyes and imagined the scene Svetlana had described — the waves, the blue bottom of the pool, even the smell of chlorine.

"Zat something else I see ees you," Svetlana continued. "Only, you're way behind me." I couldn't see Svetlana's face, but I could bet she was grinning.

"Very funny," I said and pretended to laugh.

Truth was, I felt spooked. After all, I'd just imagined Svetlana beating me. If what they say about visualization is true, didn't that make it more likely to happen? Quick! I thought to myself, I've got to come up with a new visualization — one where I win.

Before I could do that, Svetlana got up from her bench and came over to where I was standing by the lockers. Just as I'd expected, she was grinning.

Then she moved even closer, so her face was millimetres from mine — so close I could feel her breath on my skin. When I looked into her pale blue eyes, she suddenly twitched.

She's nervous, I realized. Even a strong swimmer like Svetlana can panic before a race. Maybe those visualization exercises aren't just about winning; maybe they're also supposed to help her relax.

"You seem stressed." I said. "I hope your mom's exercises help with that too."

Svetlana ignored my comment. She stared out into space as though she were trying to decide whether to say something else. Then she turned back to me and hissed, "How's your mama doing?"

I gasped.

The twitch had disappeared. Now Svetlana's eyes were gleaming as brightly as if she'd come in first after a long tough race.

But it wasn't till she snickered that I lost it.

That's when I shoved her.

She didn't see it coming. She lost her footing and slid to the ground, landing smack on her bum. If I hadn't been so angry, I might have laughed at the sight of her, sprawled on the floor, her legs sticking up in the air like some insect that had fallen from its leaf.

Svetlana scowled as she wobbled back up to her feet. "Did I say somezing wrong?" she asked, with that same nasty hiss.

My heart was beating like a drum inside my chest. What was it about Svetlana that she didn't know when to stop? I raised the palm of my hand back up towards her shoulder.

Then the locker room door swung open.

"What's wrong with you?" Clara shouted, grabbing my hand and holding it tightly in mid-air. Then she glared at both of us. "Break it up right now! You're supposed to be in the water in four minutes!"

* * *

The pool was full of waves. Just like Svetlana had described it. My heart was still pounding. I didn't know whether it was because of the fight — or because I was finally competing in the 200-metre crawl.

Our lanes were arranged according to our times, with the fastest swimmers in the middle and the slower swimmers out at the sides. Svetlana and I were in the middle; Ashley was one lane over to my right. I was relieved when I discovered that Lisa, the wide-shouldered girl from Pointe Claire who'd won the 100-metre breaststroke heat this morning, would not be competing in this event.

Swimmers were no longer crowded round their coaches' tables. Instead, they watched silently from the sidelines. The coaches' eyes were on the pool — or their stopwatches. Even the stands were quiet. Everyone knew that only this afternoon's fastest swimmers would make it to the provincials.

I hooked my toes onto the edge of the starting board. Somebody coughed. Probably Ashley. Before I could check to see if she was okay, the buzzer sounded and all 10 of us dove into the water.

Two hundred metres is eight laps in our pool — longer than a sprint, but way shorter than some of the other races. I had to pace myself, but also push hard.

The first lap was over in no time — seven left, I thought, as I tucked in my chin and pulled my knees into my chest for the flip turn. You're doing fine, I told myself, as I stretched my arms out into the water and pulled back with all my strength.

Svetlana and I were neck and neck. But I'd lost sight of Ashley.

Six, then five ... then four laps left. Just as I was about to begin my fifth lap, I spotted Ashley. She was lagging behind, still finishing up her fourth lap.

During my next lap I started to realize something was wrong. Ashley was now nearly two laps behind the rest of us. As I swam past her, I noticed how she kept bobbing to the surface for air. Why wasn't she holding her breath the way Madame Lalonde had taught us? Come on Ash! I thought, wishing she could read my mind. Push!

I didn't let myself stop to breathe until I'd taken three more strokes. When I did come up for air, the sharp smell of chlorine nearly made me gag.

Ashley had swum farther, but even so, she was only on her fifth lap. With just one lap left, all I could think about was winning. Svetlana had lost time in her last flip turn and though I couldn't be sure, I thought I might be in the lead. Yes! I thought. Yes!

Suddenly, I sensed some strange movement behind me. As I dipped my face into the water, I craned my neck so I could look behind me. Svetlana was swimming across my lane. She seemed to be heading for the other side of the pool. And she was swimming awfully fast. What on Earth was she thinking?

But I didn't have time to figure that out. Not with less than half a lap left.

I reached forward. Up ahead, I could just make out the ledge of the pool.

"You won!" an unfamiliar voice called out as I reached up for the ledge. It was an official — a dad from one of the other teams.

Nobody shouted from the stands, nor did Madame Lalonde or the other kids on the team.

Everyone was looking at the far end of the pool. I followed their gaze. Hunched over the side of the pool, wheezing as if she'd never stop, was Ashley. Svetlana was beside her, her arm around Ashley's back.

18

Visiting a Friend

There's nothing to be sorry about, silly," Ashley said. She was lying in bed, still recovering from yesterday's asthma attack. The pool had more chlorine than usual, and the doctor believed that had triggered the attack.

The wall next to Ashley's bed was covered with magazine cut-outs of cats. Kind of odd considering that besides having asthma, Ashley was allergic to cats.

"I'm your best friend. I should've been the one to stop the way—" I couldn't bring myself to say Svetlana's name.

"I was surprised when she did that," Ashley said, coughing at the end of her sentence.

"I still feel bad," I said. Even if Ashley didn't think I needed to apologize, I did. Truth was, I hadn't even thought about stopping to check on her — not when I had a chance of winning the race. "Something happens to me when I compete," I said, searching for the right words. "It's like nothing else matters."

"That's what's supposed to happen," Ashley said, reaching behind her to adjust the pillows. They had cats on them, too.

"Here, let me help," I offered, getting up from my spot at the end of her bed. "Can I get you some water or something?"

"Don't mention the word water to me, okay?" Ashley said. "But I wouldn't mind some orange juice."

Ashley was dozing when I came back with the juice. She opened her eyes when I put the glass down on her nightstand.

"Ash," I whispered, "there's something I've been wondering about …" Now probably wasn't the best time to raise the subject, but I couldn't stop myself. I had to get it out.

Ashley opened her eyes, reached for the glass of juice and took a small sip. "Did you tell Svetlana about my mom?" I asked.

"No. No, I didn't," Ashley answered quickly. Too quickly.

I looked straight at her. "Are you sure?" I asked.

Ashley put the glass down on her nightstand and shifted forward on her pillows. "I might've mentioned something," she said, without lifting her eyes from her bedspread.

"How could you?" I asked. For a second, I wanted to shake her.

Instead, I turned my back and headed for the door.

Ashley's mom was vacuuming downstairs. "I'm trying to get rid of all the dust," she shouted over the roar of the vacuum cleaner. I grabbed my jean jacket, which was hanging over the railing.

"Thanks for stopping by, but it's probably just as well you're not staying," Ashley's mom shouted. "The doctor wants Ashley to get her rest. Besides, another girl from the team called to say she'd be dropping by later."

I didn't need to ask who that girl was.

* * *

Even though I was wearing flip-flops, I ran home. When I was about halfway, the sky, which had been a bright blue on my way over to Ashley's, suddenly turned greyish-black and it started to pour. Heavy rain — the kind we only get on hot summer days — came down in thick sheets.

I felt as changeable as the weather. At first, I'd felt guilty about not having come to Ashley's rescue, but now I was furious! Ashley must've known Svetlana was the last person on Earth I wanted to let know about my mom's disappearance. How could she have been so inconsiderate? She had lots of good qualities, but keeping secrets wasn't one of them.

The angrier I felt, the faster I ran. But when I stopped at our front door and reached for my key, I wasn't sure who I was really angry at.

Truth was, I was angry with everybody. My mom for disappearing, my dad for not doing more to find her, Ashley for being such a blabbermouth, Svetlana for so many things I couldn't count them all … I was even angry at Matt for not standing up to Svetlana. Every part of me was filled with anger.

I looked at my reflection in our front window and saw the angry girl I'd expected — my flushed face, fierce-looking eyes and lined forehead. But when I looked again I spotted something else.

Sadness.

I turned away as quickly as I could.

"Abigail! Are you here?" I called out as I unlocked the door.

Abigail didn't answer. Maybe she was doing errands. Just then, I heard her voice. She said something I couldn't make out, followed by the word "Missus."

A tingle of excitement shot through my body. Abigail always called my mom "Missus." Could she be home?

"Mom!" I called out as I raced into the kitchen.

I saw Abigail's back (she was wearing a checkered blouse), but no sign of anyone else. When she turned around I realized she was on the phone.

"Let me talk to her!" I cried, nearly knocking the receiver from Abigail's hands.

But when I held it to my ear, all I heard was a crackling sound. Whoever was on the other end had hung up.

19

Another Table for Two

You forgot to take off your apron," I whispered to Abigail when she hung her raincoat on the back of her chair. We'd come for soup at Hoai Huong, the Vietnamese restaurant on Victoria Ave.

Without saying a word, Abigail untied the apron, folded it into a neat square and slipped it into her bag.

This was the first time she and I had ever eaten out together. As a rule, she disapproved of restaurants. "Hmph," she'd grunt if we mentioned food made in anyone else's kitchen but hers. Abigail didn't suffer from low self-esteem when it came to her cooking.

"Okay, Abigail," I said after we'd each ordered the house specialty, a large bowl of Tonkinoise soup — beef broth served over a huge pile of vermicelli noodles. "What's going on?"

When I insisted on knowing who'd been on the phone, Abigail had suggested we go out for lunch. "Why can't you tell me now?" I'd demanded, stamping my foot, but Abigail had led me by the shoulder over to the kitchen table. From the way she'd treated me, you'd think I was a kid having a tantrum, not a girl whose mother had been missing for ten days.

"Some things," Abigail had said, "are better discussed over a bowl of soup." But I had a feeling she was just stalling.

Even now, Abigail wasn't eager to talk. I could tell from the way she kept folding and unfolding her napkin.

"She made me promise not to say anything," she said at last.

"You mean Mom, right?" I was determined to get the story straight.

"Yes," Abigail said, lifting one finger to her lips when the waiter arrived with two bowls of steaming soup. Fresh basil floated on the surface of each bowl.

Once the waiter returned to his spot behind the ceramic Buddha near the cash register, Abigail continued. "Your mom has phoned three times since she disappeared. She's fine, but says that she needs some time away from … I mean, some time on her own. She made me promise not to tell you," Abigail said, dabbing her forehead with her napkin. "I told her you're going to the provincials," she added, I could tell she wanted to end this fast.

The information Abigail had let slip wiped out the comfort of knowing Mom was okay. My mom needed time away from me. Somehow, knowing that made me feel worse than before.

I took a deep breath before asking my next question. "Where is she?"

"She won't say."

"Well, where do you think she is?" Abigail sure wasn't making this easy.

"I'd say Vancouver."

"Ahh," I said, more to myself than to Abigail, "where the little boy drowned."

"You know about that?" Abigail asked, looking up anxiously from her bowl of soup.

"I know how a boy drowned in Vancouver when my mom was life guarding. And I know she disappeared on the twenty-fifth anniversary of his death."

Abigail didn't say a word, but when she put down her spoon, her hands were shaking. "I should have realized the anniversary was … She never wanted you to know," she said. "Who told you?" she asked a second later, her voice rising.

I couldn't think of anyone to blame, so I told the truth. "Nobody. I read about it."

Abigail looked puzzled.

"I found an old newspaper article in her nightstand."

"What were you doing in there?" Abigail exclaimed. Obviously, she'd stopped worrying about being overheard.

"I was looking for clues. You know, Abigail, she *is* my mom."

This time, when Abigail looked at me, she didn't seem angry. "I know," she said, reaching for my hand.

"Were you working for my mom's family when he drowned?" I asked.

For a few minutes, Abigail said nothing. The faraway look in her eyes told me she was remembering back 25 years. "Your mother and I were still close, even though she was already a teenager. She blamed herself for that child's death. Weeks passed before she'd even come out of her room. I brought her food — all her favourites — but she hardly ate."

"Your dad was the one who helped her through. They really became close that summer. They got married five years later, but every spring, she'd have trouble again. Your dad thought moving to Montreal would help. And it did — for a while — but then she got bad again."

"Why didn't she want me to know?" I asked.

"From the time you were a baby, she knew you loved water. When we'd give you a bath, you'd cry when we drained the water. She was proud that you turned out to be a good swimmer. Your mother didn't want to do anything that would take away the good feelings you got in the water."

As Abigail spoke, I pictured my mom watching me from the stands — the way she had for so many years. I remembered how she'd wave when I looked up at her. But somehow, she always seemed sad at the same time. Had she been remembering the accident?

Slowly, I was beginning to understand how much it must have taken for my mom to let me race.

20

Boy Trouble

"Eet was stupid of you to help zat girl. Very stupid."

"I was vorried about her."

"Vorry about yourself."

Technically, I wasn't listening in. I just happened to be reaching down to tie my shoelace when Svetlana's rusty car with the cleaning service sign screeched into the parking lot.

The car windows were wide open and I could hear every word Svetlana and her mother were saying. I could have hurried up and finished tying my shoelace, but by then, I wanted to hear the rest. So I stayed bent down behind a parked van, pretending to tie the other shoe.

Though I'm not exactly fond of Svetlana, I thought it was wrong for her mom to call her stupid. My mom would never talk to me like that. On the other hand, my mom had taken off because she needed a break from me. At least Svetlana's mom was around for her daughter.

"Vat if something bad had happened to zee girl?" Svetlana asked.

"Nothing bad vud have happened," her mother said impatiently, as if she was tired of making the same point. "Helping zat girl was zee coach's job, not yours. You have one job, Svetlana — to vin. And not just for you."

"I have to vin for you, too," Svetlana said in a voice that sounded like it was coming from a robot.

"Zat's right," her mother said, sounding calmer. "Svetlana, you spoiled your chance to qualify for zee crawl, but at least you qualified for zee breaststroke. Zat's what we have to concentrate on now."

"Yes, mama," Svetlana said in that same robotic voice.

"Now go svim," Svetlana's mother said. Since that seemed to be the end of the conversation, I stood up and started for the door leading into the sports complex. I could see the backs of their two blonde heads.

When Svetlana's mother leaned over to kiss her daughter, I felt an ache in my throat. I remembered how, a couple of weeks ago, I'd pushed my mom away when I'd woken up and found her sitting on my bed. As for Svetlana, she avoided her mother's kiss by popping out of the car. A second later, the car screeched away, a thick cloud of blue smoke trailing behind it.

"Looks like that car is burning oil," I heard a voice say. Matt was coming up from behind me.

"My mama has to bring it in for an up-tune," Svetlana said. The three of us had reached the door at about the same time.

"An up-tune?" Matt and I asked. "You mean a tune-up!" we added a moment later, both figuring out at the same time what Svetlana had meant.

"Yes, a tune-up. Zat's it," Svetlana laughed, holding the door open for us. "Hey, Barracuda," Svetlana said, glancing at me as she spoke. "Vant to go for ice cream after practice?"

For a second, Matt rocked back and forth on the balls of his feet. "Na, I can't," he said, without looking up at her.

"You can't?" Svetlana seemed surprised.

Matt looked at me as though he needed help. I just shrugged.

"Look, Svetlana," Matt said slowly, "I can't. Plus, I don't

want to."

I winced. He could have let her down more gently.

In a way, I admired Svetlana for going after what she wanted. But if you go ahead and tell someone how you feel about them, you take a chance they'll reject you — like Matt just did. Maybe it was safer to hide your feelings.

"You don't vant to?" Svetlana asked.

Something in her voice told me she was about to cry.

* * *

Some people wail when they cry, with big wet tears running down their cheeks and lots of sound effects. Other people weep quietly, but their shoulders shake as if they're having trouble keeping hold of their emotions. Svetlana stood in front of her locker whimpering like a dog that had been locked out of the house.

I would've figured if my arch-enemy, the girl who'd been my rival for the last two years, was crying, I'd be happy. Only I wasn't.

I pretended not to notice, but that got harder as she kept whimpering.

Just as I was debating whether to say something, Svetlana turned to face me. "So do you vant to know what's wrong or not?" she asked.

"Sure," I said, trying to force my lips into a smile, but not quite managing it.

"Everyzing," she said. "Everyzing is wrong."

"I know what you mean," I told her.

"You do?" Svetlana asked. "So vat do you do when you feel like that?"

Finally, a question I could answer. "I swim."

21

A Weird Conversation

W e're going to work on our pulls today," Madame Lalonde shouted, passing us each a pair of plastic paddles. "As you know, if you don't pull properly during the crawl, these paddles will slow you down. Just remember — extend your arm for the longest possible pull; relax it, then reach and give me another strong, quick pull underwater." Madame Lalonde demonstrated from the deck, her biceps rippling as she made an arc in the air.

I slipped my wrist through the loop at the bottom of the paddle and slid my middle finger into the top loop. Hand paddles make you feel like a duck, though I figure webbed feet are easier to maneuver than these things. If Ashley had been around — and if we hadn't been in a fight — we'd have waited for Madame Lalonde to turn her back, and then we'd have made quacking noises at each other.

But Ashley wasn't at practice. The doctor had insisted she take a week off from swimming.

Svetlana was having trouble with one of her paddles. "Need a hand?" I offered, wading towards her. Of course, my hands weren't exactly available.

"I zink I have it," Svetlana said as she forced her middle finger into the loop.

"One hundred metres of crawl. Let's go!" Madame Lalonde shouted, blowing her whistle.

This time, I didn't start swimming right after Matt the way I usually did. I had to take care of something first — and I wasn't looking forward to it.

"You did the right thing by helping Ashley," I told Svetlana, before I pushed off into the water. There, I said it. I was glad I hadn't given her time to answer. My head was already dropping underwater, but from the corner of my eye, I saw Svetlana smile.

Usually, Svetlana smirks. Yes, that's the word for it, I decided, as I approached the other end of the pool. Whenever she does that — and she does it a lot — you feel like she's laughing at you. But just now, she hadn't smirked — she'd smiled. Definitely.

Suddenly, I remembered something my art teacher had told us — how a smile is the first form of communication between a baby and his mother.

What I'd give right now, I thought, to see my mom's smile. For a second, I let myself float in the water, weightless, imagining her smile. The corners of her mouth turned up just a little, her eyes half-closed.

The sound of Madame Lalonde's whistle brought me back to the exercise. Reach, pull, extend, then reach again...

But now my mind returned to Svetlana. Maybe she isn't so bad, I thought as I prepared for my flip turn and the bottoms of my feet touched the wall. But once I was right side up again, I began remembering everything Svetlana had ever done to bug me. Her voice echoed inside my head, asking, "How's your mama?" and "Did I say somezing wrong?"

Reach and pull, I told myself as I forced myself to focus on the paddles.

I felt a rush of water coming from behind me as I completed the next lap. Svetlana was following me, so that had to be her tapping my shoulder as I completed the next flip turn. "What?" I asked, turning to face her.

Svetlana was bobbing in the water, her upturned nose pointing at the ceiling. "My mama's angry with me for helping Ashley," she said before her head disappeared back under the water.

I slowed down and moved in closer to the rope, knowing that if I gave her room, Svetlana wouldn't be able to resist the chance to pass me. As she came closer, I timed my movements so we'd be lifting our heads to breathe at the same time. "She shouldn't be angry," I said, sputtering from the strain of holding my face out of the water and talking at the same time.

I was surprised when Svetlana kept pace with me, rather than moving ahead. To make sure, I slowed down. So did Svetlana. "My mama cares only about vinning," she said as we neared the other end of the pool.

One lap left. This, I thought, has got to be the weirdest conversation I've ever had. Even though it was my turn to say something, I didn't. Instead, I tried to concentrate on my pulls. Svetlana's eyes met mine the next time I lifted my head out of the water. You could tell she was waiting for me to say something.

"I miss my mother," I said. I hadn't planned to say it. The words had just spilled out. As soon as they were out, I started regretting them. I hadn't meant to confide in Svetlana.

I plunged my head under the water. I felt safer here. Here, at least, there were no words. But at that very moment, Svetlana did something totally weird. She reached underwater and grabbed my hand. I was going to pull it away, but before I could, she gave it a squeeze.

When we neared the edge of the pool, Svetlana pushed ahead,

completing her 100 metres about a second and a half before me. Leave it to Svettie, I thought, to get competitive during a paddling exercise. Was that her mother's influence? I wondered.

"Looks like we both have mother trouble," I said when I joined her at the side of the pool.

This time, Madame Lalonde's whistle interrupted our conversation. "Quit gabbing! This is swim team, not a tea party!" she shouted. Then she looked down at the two of us and shook her head. "Wonders never cease," she muttered. "I've never had to ask you two to stop talking."

22

Downtown

Yes?" the receptionist asked, looking up from her computer screen with a tight smile. I knew from the way she kept glancing back at her keyboard that she thought I was a nuisance.

"I'm here for Mr. Miller." I kept my hands in my pockets as I spoke.

It was Wednesday afternoon, which meant I had a free period after lunch.

The way the receptionist looked at me, starting first with my feet and slowly making her way up to the top of my head, made me feel self-conscious about what I was wearing — sneakers, cut-off shorts, a grey tank top and an Expos baseball cap.

"Do you have an appointment?" she asked, looking down at her fingernails, which were polished a silvery pink. Her white blouse was buttoned to the neck. "Mr. Miller is a busy man."

"I know," I said. "That's why I'm here. He's my dad and I have to talk to him."

I'd begun to learn that sometimes, when something's really upsetting you, it's better to let it out. Problems have a way of getting bigger when you keep them inside. In the end, I didn't regret confronting Ashley about her having told Svetlana about my mom. Sure, I was upset when I stormed out of her house, but we straightened it out a couple of days later. She called me

to apologize for blabbing to Svetlana, and I apologized for losing my temper. I was glad I'd told her how I felt. If I hadn't,
those angry feelings would just have grown inside me.

Now it was my dad's turn. I wanted him to know I'd had it
with family secrets.

For a few seconds, the receptionist didn't say a thing. She
just stared at me; her jaw dropped. "Of course, I'll let him know
you're here. Victoria, isn't it? You don't look anything like your
picture."

She pressed a button at the bottom of her telephone. "Sir,"
she said without lifting the receiver, "Your daughter's here to
see you."

"She is?" Dad's voice crackled over the intercom. "Tell her
I'll be right out, Judith."

"You don't look like him," Judith observed. Now that she
knew I was the boss's daughter, she seemed to forget whatever
she'd been working on. I decided I liked her better when she
was trying to get rid of me. "You don't have his hair — or his
colouring."

"People say I have his eyes."

Judith peered into my eyes as though I were some stuffed owl
on display at a museum. "They're right," she concluded. "Your
eyes are the same shade of grey."

Luckily, my dad came out of his office before Judith could
continue inspecting me. "What a pleasant surprise!" he said,
reaching his arm out towards me. "Come on in."

I'd hadn't been in my dad's office since I was little. He still
had the same cherrywood desk, but somehow, when I was
smaller, it had seemed bigger. Two stacks of file folders were
piled on the desk, one so big it looked as though it might topple
over at any minute.

I glanced around the room. Floor-to-ceiling windows looked

out over downtown. From up here on the twentieth floor, the cars and people below us were just specks.

My eyes continued to survey the room, landing on a long table across from the desk. There, in a Lucite frame, was a photo I hadn't seen in ages — the one that had been in the window of the camera store so many years ago. I stared at the image of Mom, Dad and me, hanging on to each other like monkeys. No wonder Judith hadn't recognized me.

"Can I get you something?" my dad asked, reaching for his telephone. "A Coke?"

I ignored his questions. "Don't you want to know why I'm here?" I asked, lifting my head to look into his eyes. They *were* the same shade as mine.

Dad let go of the phone and turned to gaze out the window. "Go ahead," he said when he looked back at me, "tell me."

"For one thing," I began, "you don't know me. You don't even know what time I'm supposed to get home after a bowling party. For another thing, you're never home. And when you are, you hardly ever have time to talk — not with all your paperwork and your cell phone ringing all the time." As I heard myself speak — my voice louder and higher than usual — I realized I sounded like a nagging wife.

Hey, I wondered, had my mom been upset about these things, too? For the first time, it occurred to me that maybe Mom's disappearance wasn't all about me; maybe she'd needed a break from Dad, too.

"Now Vic, you have to underst—" my dad started to say, but I didn't let him finish his sentence. I had a feeling if I didn't say everything I wanted to say right now, I might never say it. Not just because I practically had to schedule an appointment to talk to Dad, but more because I thought I might chicken out.

"I know about Mom and Avery Munro. And I know you

knew Mom when Avery drowned and that was why you ended up leaving Vancouver. And I know Mom's been phoning Abigail. But what I really can't stand — besides the fact that I've got a mom who took off without saying good-bye and a workaholic dad—" and here, I took a deep breath, not just because I needed to come up for air, but also because I had a feeling that if I didn't, I might start to cry, "is that in our family, nobody — nobody — ever tells me anything!"

"Did Abigail tell you about the drowning?" my dad asked. His eyes had clouded over, the way they do when he's about to lose his temper.

"No, she didn't. I read about it in this newspaper clipping I found in Mom's nightstand."

"You shouldn't have been snooping in there."

"Don't you see, Dad? That's not the point. The point is we've been playing some weird charade. We live in this nice house and you have this big company, and I might even get to be a prize-winning swimmer some day, but we're *not* perfect," I said, gesturing towards the photo on the table across from his desk. "We're in trouble, Dad — and we need to stop acting like we aren't."

Dad leaned back into his chair and sighed. For the first time, I noticed little lines near the corners of his eyes. "Okay," he said.

"Okay, what?"

"Okay, you're right."

That didn't make me feel much better. "So what do we now?" I asked.

"We start with this," my dad said, getting up from his chair and walking to the other side of his desk where I was sitting. Then he leaned down and kissed the top of my head. "I'm sorry, Vic," he whispered. "Mom and I wanted to protect you. Though I never realized it till just now, I guess we were really trying to protect ourselves — from the past and from our memories of Avery's death. Those were terrible days and the newspaper coverage only made things worse for us," he said, rubbing his fingers against his temples.

"Then somehow, when we weren't looking, you started growing up and you stopped needing that kind of protection. You started needed something else — something like the truth, I guess — but we weren't strong enough to give it to you."

I didn't cry when Dad told me Mom had disappeared. I didn't cry when Abigail let it slip she thought Mom needed a break from me. I didn't cry when I fought with Svetlana or Ashley, and I didn't cry when I told Dad why I was upset.

But I cried now. Big wet tears. The weird thing was that when they landed on my lips, they didn't taste salty. They tasted like chlorine.

23

Jitters

Go Fish!" Ashley called out, puckering her lips as she did her fish imitation.

"Rats!" I said, drawing another card from the deck on the table.

"Do you realize," Ashley asked, rolling her eyes, "how cutthroat you are? We're playing cards — not competing in a swim meet."

"Glug, glug," I said. "Your turn."

"Being competitive isn't always bad," my dad joined in. "It happens to have served me well."

He was sitting with us in the den, in an armchair by the fireplace.

"Aren't you supposed to be working on a crossword?" I asked him.

"I didn't know you were into crosswords," Ashley said, turning towards my dad.

"I used to be. Before life got so busy. They're a good way to relax," Dad said, returning to the puzzle on his lap.

"Got any fours?" Ashley asked me.

"How did you know?" I turned over all three of them.

"Fish upon a wish! Hope you're not too upset, Vic, but I just beat you."

I was trying to decide if I *was* upset, when Dad's cell phone rang.

"William Miller here," I said at the same time as Dad.

Ashley grinned at me.

"I see," Dad said. "In other words, if we don't make a bid tonight, we risk losing the deal. Don't worry. I'll meet you at the office in fifteen minutes," he said, pausing to check his watch.

Dad practically leapt out of his armchair. "So much for relaxing. Blame my competitive nature, but I'd hate to miss out on this one. I'll be back by 11:00. You'd better get to bed before then, Vic. You need your rest for the provincials tomorrow. What time are you waking up?"

"Five a.m. But you can sleep till five-thirty."

"I'll see you in the morning then."

"I'd better get going too," Ashley said. Though she hadn't qualified, she was coming along to cheer for the rest of us. "Sorry I can't give you a chance to beat me at Fish!"

"I'll take you home, Ashley. But we need to leave straightaway," Dad said.

* * *

"Better pack your gym bag," I said out loud. Even the sound of my own voice was better than the eerie stillness.

As I headed upstairs, I thought about Dad's competitiveness. Maybe I'm more like him than I realized.

But being competitive and acting as though things were perfect wasn't working for Dad. It hadn't kept Mom home, that's for sure.

I unhooked my bathing suit from the plastic hanger on the shower curtain rod. Why does winning matter so much to me?

Part of me didn't even want to compete tomorrow. Part of me

wanted to sleep in — or run away. Not to a beach, where there'd only be more swimming. No, the Arctic would be a better bet.

I reached into the closet for a towel. Competing's just something I do automatically.

Where was my lucky bathing cap anyway? Not in my gym bag, where it was supposed to be.

She gave it to me — and I wanted it. Even if I don't race tomorrow, I need that cap.

I thought about Mom and the Arctic. Maybe the part of me that wants to escape comes from her.

Must be in my locker, I thought as I checked the time. Nearly 8:15. The sports complex is open till 9:00 p.m. But I need to leave straightaway.

But I need to leave straightaway. Isn't that what Dad said before he left? I scribbled him a note in case he got home early and was worried about where I was. As I dropped the note on the hallway floor, I couldn't help wondering: was I turning into my parents?

24

Decisions

I rubbed the soft nylon between my fingers. I'd found the bathing cap at the bottom of my locker. It must've fallen out of my gym bag.

But I wasn't ready to go home. I needed to think, so I went to the pool. Luckily, no one was there. I took off my sneakers and socks and dipped my feet in the water. I hadn't done that since I was little.

Was I going to compete tomorrow? Or had swimming stopped being fun? Why give up when I had a chance of winning at the provincials? Or was I some sort of machine, driven by pure competition?

If I sat there long enough, maybe I'd be able to decide.

I felt a hand on my shoulder. Startled — even scared — I turned around. Whoever it was had used the entrance behind me. I saw the mop of curly hair first. Hair like mine. Then I smelled lavender.

"Hello, honey." She knelt down beside me. "I'm so sorry," my mother whispered.

I had to touch her to make sure she was real — not some mirage like the one I'd had before. She opened her arms to hug me, longer even than the hug Svetlana gave Matt.

"How'd you know I was here?" I asked.

"From your note. All I could think about on the plane was how I had to talk to you first. Honey, I'm so sorry … for every-thing. For getting sick, for going away—"

"Without saying good-bye," I reminded her.

"Without saying good-bye," she said, nodding her head.

Then Mom took off her shoes and socks and dipped her feet into the water, too. "I was gone," she said, bumping her foot against mine.

I bumped my foot back against hers. "I figured that part out."

"That isn't … what I meant," she said. "My heart … and my mind were gone. It was never about you."

"I thought you needed a break from me and Dad."

"I thought so, too. Being a mom's a huge responsibility and sometimes, it's scary. And you know how Dad is. He and I need to work a few things out. I really needed a break from myself — only that's impossible."

"You seem good," I told her.

"I'm much better. But I can't ever be like I was before. What about you, sweetheart? How you doing?"

"Okay," I said, "better now that you're back. I was worried, and I've been upset about others things, too."

"Like what?"

"Swimming. I'm beginning to think I inherited Dad's com-petitiveness — and your wanting to run away. It's a bad combination."

"You want to run away?" Mom's eyebrows arched in sur-prise.

"Sometimes. To the Arctic."

Mom kicked my foot again with hers. "Because there's no swimming — unless you're a penguin?"

"I don't know if I even want to race tomorrow."

"It's the provincials, isn't it? That's why I came home tonight, so I could be there tomorrow. *If* you compete."

"How do I decide?"

"You'll just know. It sounds to me like you're drowning."

I didn't expect Mom to use that word. "I know about Avery," I whispered.

"I went to Vancouver to see his family."

"How are they?" I asked.

"They're okay," she said. "They say they never blamed me for his death. Avery's mom's never forgiven herself for losing sight of him that day. You know, I think forgiving yourself is harder than forgiving someone else. We should've told you about Avery—"

"Mom," I said, thinking about what she'd just said. "It's time to forgive yourself."

She smiled as she looked into my eyes. "When you were small, you adored water. The bathtub … the wading pool ... the sprinkler. On rainy days, you used to run around outside in your bathing suit. You were so excited when you learned to swim, and when you won your first race. But maybe joining the swim team wasn't a good idea. Still, I think if you love something, you should do it. Do you still love to swim — and race?"

I did a little flutter kick and inhaled deeply, so I could smell the chlorine. I looked up at the flags hanging over the pool and that made me remember the excitement I feel during a competition. And I thought of feeling like a fish in the water.

"I think so."

We dried our feet with the towel I'd brought from my locker. Mom reached for my hand and pulled me up to the deck.

"You know something, Mom? You might've just prevented a drowning."

25

Feeling Like a Fish

The water temperature was perfect. Not too hot, not too cold. Just right. For a second, I felt like Goldilocks tasting Baby Bear's porridge. When I dove underwater, all I could see was murky darkness. I stretched out one arm, pulling back hard, then the other.

Ahh, I thought as I kicked my feet, there's nothing like a lake.

Mom, Dad and I were spending a week in a log cabin in the Laurentians, an hour north of Montreal. They'd insisted on a place by a lake. Even lying in bed and looking out my window, I could see it — big, blue and beautiful. And because it was the middle of July, the lake was as warm as bathwater.

Mom and Dad were sitting on the dock, talking like they'd been doing since we arrived on Sunday.

I was headed for the far end. My body felt like it needed a long swim. I thought about how my technique had improved since the fall. I was diving in more deeply, stretching further with my arms, and I'd pretty much mastered the flip turn.

But I hadn't won the race and I wasn't going to the nationals.

At least, not this year.

Images of the day came back to me as I switched from crawl into breaststroke.

Ashley's face when she saw Mom in the car that morning. "Mrs. Miller," she'd said, trying to act normal. "Is it ever good to see you!"

A girl from an East End team who was so nervous she threw up on the deck before her race.

Me on the starting block, my lower legs trembling.

Mom and Dad waving from the stands. Dad's jeans and a T-shirt making him look younger than usual. For a second, I could imagine them as a young couple, working together at a Vancouver pool.

Next came an image of the end of my race. A girl from a Saguenay-Lac St. Jean team only a few centimetres ahead of me. Focus, I'd told myself.

But I just couldn't push myself hard enough.

Matt won in his category. And Svetlana in hers.

I wasn't as upset as I thought I'd be, though it did occur to me that Matt and Svetlana would be traveling together to Calgary in August.

After the award ceremony and the photos, Svetlana threw her arm around my shoulders and whispered, "Vat do you think of Juan?"

"Juan?"

"I never noticed how cute he ees."

Matt was waiting outside the girls' locker room. "Hey, Vic," he said, shuffling from one foot to the other, "Can I ask you something?"

"Sure. What's up?"

"I was wondering — well — wanna go to a movie sometime?"

I stared into his eyes. "Are you asking because you feel sorry for me?"

Matt shuffled some more. "No," he said, "I've liked you all along. I guess I was just scared."

"Okay, then, yes. But I've gotta go and meet my mom and dad. Call me."

Matt's face brightened. "I know you said you were too young to date, but we could say it was a get-tog—"

"You know something, Matt? I said that in April." I smiled into his eyes, which were smiling back. "A lot of stuff has changed since then."

A sleek black fish brought my mind back to the present — and to the lake. He darted off ahead of me, his back fins shifting from side to side.

That looks like fun, I thought, as I dove deeper into the water, and swiveled from one hip to the other. I'd never felt more like a fish.

Other books you'll enjoy in the Sports Stories series

Figure Skating

❏ *A Stroke of Luck* by Kathryn Ellis #6
Strange accidents are stalking one of the skaters at the Millwood Arena.

❏ *The Winning Edge* by Michele Martin Bossley #28
Jennie wants more than anything to win a gruelling series of competitions, but is success worth losing her friends?

❏ *Leap of Faith* by Michele Martin Bossley #36
Amy wants to win at any cost, until an injury makes skating almost impossible. Will she go on?

Gymnastics

❏ *The Perfect Gymnast* by Michele Martin Bossley #9
Abby's new friend has all the confidence she needs, but she also has a serious problem that nobody but Abby seems to know about.

Riding

❏ *A Way with Horses* by Peter McPhee #11
A young Alberta rider, invited to study show jumping at a posh local riding school, uncovers a secret.

❏ *Riding Scared* by Marion Crook #15
A reluctant new rider struggles to overcome her fear of horses.

❏ *Katie's Midnight Ride* by C. A. Forsyth #16
An ambitious barrel racer finds herself without a horse weeks before her biggest rodeo.

❏ *Glory Ride* by Tamara L. Williams #21
Chloe Anderson fights memories of a tragic fall for a place on the Ontario Young Riders Team.

❏ *Cutting It Close* by Marion Crook #24
In this novel about barrel racing, a young rider finds her horse is in trouble just as she's about to compete in an important event.

❏ *Shadow Ride* by Tamara L. Williams #37
Bronwen has to choose between competing aggressively for herself or helping out a teammate.

Swimming

❏ *Breathing Not Required* by Michele Martin Bossley #4
Gracie works so hard to be chosen for the solo at synchronized swimming that she almost loses her best friend in the process.

❏ *Water Fight!* by Michele Martin Bossley #14
Josie's perfect sister is driving her crazy, but when she takes up swimming — Josie's sport — it's too much to take.

❏ *Taking a Dive* by Michele Martin Bossley #19
Josie holds the provincial record for the butterfly, but in this sequel to Water Fight! she can't seem to match her own time and might not go on to the nationals.

❏ *Great Lengths* by Sandra Diersch #26
Fourteen-year-old Jessie decides to find out whether the rumours about a new swimmer at her Vancouver club are true.

❏ *Pool Princess* by Michele Martin Bossley #47
In this sequel to *Breathing Not Required*, Gracie must deal with a bully on the new synchro team in Calgary.

❏ *Flip Turn* by Monique Polak #67
Swimmer Victoria Miller has been training intently to keep up with her teammate and rival, Svetlana. When Victoria's family situation takes a grim turn, she finds help where she least expects it.